Next to the front door stood a pine writing desk with a phone, a reservation book, and an answering machine. Reaching out, Margaret pushed the blinking red message button.

"Hey, it's Lauren, I'm gonna be late. I got an audition at ten," said a careless, cigarette-sucking voice.

"I must stop hiring actresses," Margaret muttered.

"You've got to stick with the older ones that never work," said Lilly.

There was a sharp bang at the back door, followed by a gust of cool air and, finally, Clarissa Richardson. Beautiful and just a gasp from forty, she favored theatrical attire and Bakelite bracelets.

Without so much as a hello, she breezed in with the day's dilemma.

"My cell is almost dead and my agent's supposed to call!" Rummaging through her bulging purse, she spilled a pair of eyeglasses on the floor.

Lilly playfully scooped up the emerald-green frames and dangled them in her face. "When did you start wearing these?"

Clarissa snatched them back. "They're for driving."

"Uh-oh! Can estrogen replacement be far behind?"

"What are you talking about? I'm still in my thirties."

Is that in dog years? Lilly thought.

SANDRA HARPER

High Tea

POCKET BOOKS

NEW YORK   LONDON   TORONTO   SYDNEY

Pocket Books
A Division of Simon & Schuster, Inc.
1230 Avenue of the Americas
New York, NY 10020

First Pocket Books trade paperback edition November 2008

POCKET and colophon are registered trademarks of Simon & Schuster, Inc.

For information about special discounts for bulk purchases,
please contact Simon & Schuster Special Sales at
1-800-456-6798 or business@simonandschuster.com

Designed by Jan Pisciotta

Manufactured in the United States of America

1   3   5   7   9   10   8   6   4   2

Library of Congress Cataloging-in-Publication Data

Harper, Sandra A.
High tea / by Sandra A. Harper.
p. cm.
1. Tearooms—Fiction. 2. Middle-aged women—Fiction.
3. British—California—Los Angeles—Fiction. 4. Los Angeles
(Calif.)—Fiction. I. Title.
PS3608.A776H54 2008
813'.6—dc22
2008014549

Adapted from the play *Magpie's Tearoom* by Sandra A. Harper.

ISBN-13: 978-1-4165-8062-1
ISBN-10: 1-4165-8062-X

For Eric

Acknowledgments

Thanks to my agent, Nicole Gregory, and my editor, Kathy Sagan, who believe in me and this book and are simply the best gals ever. To my writing group, Greg Chandler, Michael Gross, Lori Gunnell, and Peggy Miley for their great notes, good food, and encouragement.

To Tracy Tynan, who has been there, from start to finish, and whose wit, wisdom, and egg salad are an inspiration. To Kerry Madden for expert advice and Norma Acland, Julia Jones, and Christine Cluley for English lessons. To Chado and The Cook's Library for many lovely hours of research.

And finally, to Jackson and Eric, the men in my life . . . could you learn to like tea?

Magpie's Tearoom

High Tea

Choice of Tea

English Breakfast: The classic blend of Assam, Ceylon, and Chinese leaves. Perfect with milk.

Earl Grey: Smoky and distinctive. Flavored with oil of Bergamot.

Cameroon: An African specialty, malty and aromatic. Served in the Court of England.

Jasmine: Silvery and elegant, with fragrant floral notes.

Chamomile: Calming and soothing. Best with lemon and honey.

Sandwiches

Cucumber and Sweet Butter, Watercress Dill, Egg Salad, French Ham and Marmalade, Scottish Salmon and Cream Cheese, Chicken Curry

---

Scones

Our traditional English Scones served with Devon Cream and Strawberry Jam

---

Sweets

Luscious Coconut Cake, Lemon Tart, Fresh Strawberries, Buttery Shortbread, Petits Fours

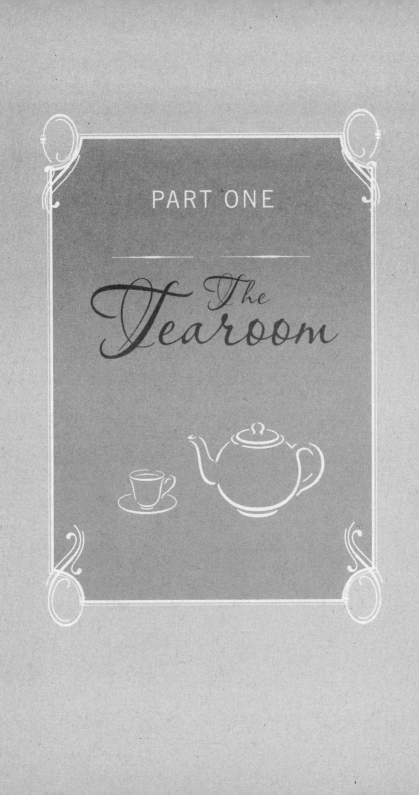

PART ONE

The Tearoom

Chapter One

Magpie's Tearoom was a lovely refuge from modern life.

Nestled between a travel bookstore and a vintage clothing boutique, it had survived Nouvelle Cuisine, Low Carbs, and Raw Food. Although there were few damp, drizzly days in Los Angeles, there was always a warm welcoming fire at Magpie's to suggest otherwise.

Pictures of sporting dogs and the bucolic English countryside hung on the rosy pink walls. A towering china hutch displayed dainty cups and saucers with storybook patterns like Tally Ho and Chelsea Gardens. Sometimes, while relaxing in one of the worn armchairs and sipping a cup of Earl Grey, a customer would tell Margaret that owning a tearoom like Magpie's must be the most wonderful job in the world.

Of course Margaret would smile graciously.

And then pour them more tea.

On this Thursday in February, it actually *was* raining and Margaret Moore was late. Stepping off the porch of her tidy cream-colored bungalow, she hurried across the soggy lawn and then slid behind the wheel of her old Volvo. Winding down to Fountain Avenue, she immediately discovered that traffic was jammed all the way to Crescent Heights. Remembering the days of the ten-minute commute, she groaned. Now it took at least forty minutes to get anywhere in the city.

Just before 3rd Street, she turned left into the alley and pulled into one of four spaces marked Tearoom. A satin-blue Prius was parked beside her.

Lilly's on time, she thought gratefully.

With the expertise of an Englishwoman, she unfurled her umbrella and reached the back door with nary a spot of water landing on her raincoat. Her shoulder-length chestnut hair hung perfectly in place.

Marching briskly into the kitchen, she stowed her purse and umbrella on a stainless steel baker's rack. Shrugging off her coat, she noticed dirty bowls littering the counter and a pan in the sink filled with something resembling amber crystals. Then she heard the rush of running water.

She knocked on the bathroom door. "Lilly?"

A rotund woman of fifty emerged, dabbing her wet face with paper towels. "Hope you don't mind. I crashed here last night," she said.

Margaret did mind but decided not to engage in what she knew would be a lengthy conversation about Lilly's domestic problems. "As long as you don't make a habit of it," was all she said.

Several aprons and a crisp white shirt hung on hooks next to the bathroom door. Margaret exchanged her coat for a black-and-white plaid apron that complemented her narrow black slacks and long-sleeved T-shirt.

Lilly squirted some gel into her palms and spiked up her short gray hair. "Deborah and I had a fight."

She's too young for you, thought Margaret, examining the pot of burned crystals in the sink.

"Just let that soak," said Lilly. "I thought a butterscotch pudding would make an interesting trifle, but the caramel seized."

Margaret's blue-gray eyes clouded. "How can I possibly go to England and leave the tearoom under your command?"

"You're going to England?" Lilly scrubbed at an egg stain on her soiled chef's jacket. "When did this happen?"

"Nothing's planned. But my mother's getting on, you know. She's almost eighty."

"I thought you hated your mother."

Margaret drew herself up. "Where did you get that idea? Just because we're not . . . overly fussy with one another. I have enormous respect for her."

Quickly turning her attention to the kitchen, she surveyed it with dismay. Although she employed a daily cleaning service, they never seemed to scrub the sink to her satisfaction. And Lilly was the messiest chef on earth. She never closed drawers or returned utensils to their proper hook on the overhead rack. Dishes were jammed willy-nilly on the open shelves below the counters and teacups were stacked precariously in the cabinets above. It wasn't as if this were a grand restaurant, either. They were a medium-sized tearoom with a dwindling inventory of china and flatware. It was sheer luck that the Health Department hadn't caught them in this condition and slapped them with a C rating.

Lilly seized a tray of buff-colored scones. "I made these last night to go with my insomnia," she beamed. "Peanut butter chocolate chip."

"Sounds like a hideous American candy bar."

"Oh, come on, Margaret, half the world loves peanut butter and chocolate. I think we could make a killing on these."

"Must I remind you that we are not here to make a killing. We are here to serve tradition."

Abandoning the kitchen, Margaret forged on with her morning routine. Why is it so difficult for Lilly to stick to the menu, she wondered, heading down the hallway towards the tearoom. It is simply crucial to have proper scones, layer cake, and egg salad at the ready. Customers depend upon it.

At the end of the hall was a door with a small brass sign inscribed "W.C." Inside the customer restroom, blue toile wallpaper and a pedestal sink gave the space a slightly Victorian air. She checked to be sure there was tissue, hand towels, and seat covers. Noticing a small puddle of water next to the toilet, she averted her eyes and hoped it was residue from last night's mopping and not a harbinger of ugly things to come.

From there, it was three quick steps to the tearoom. She crossed the floor to the two large windows that faced 3rd Street. Gently pulling back the chintz curtains, she tied them up with ruffled sashes and glanced out at the sweeping rain. I never really wanted to leave London, she thought. That had been Tony.

Shaken by this unexpected nostalgia, she set about putting her place in order. Neither trendy—nor conservative—there was an underlying elegance in the mismatched slipcovers and scuffed hardwood floors. Club chairs and ladder-backed chairs snuggled up to the tables—all good pieces snatched at flea markets and garage sales, long before that sort of treasure hunt became a pastime for studio executives and hipsters. The choice spot in the house was the loveseat next to the fireplace. A paneled oak door on a wrought-iron base served as its tea table and a beveled mirror over the mantel captured the room in its face. All the old customers wanted this table and Margaret had honed her diplomatic skills on its availability.

As she straightened chairs and pinched dead petals off the roses in several vases, Lilly followed closely behind, not being the least bit helpful.

"We fought about this weekend. Deborah doesn't want to go away with me. She never wants to leave town!"

"She's new here. It's still exciting." Margaret glanced at her watch: ten-thirty, customers in an hour.

"She refuses to visit any more B&Bs. She hates eating breakfast with retired couples in matching jogging suits."

"Can you blame her?"

"No." Lilly stuck out her lower lip. "But don't most couples like to go away on romantic weekends?"

Margaret rearranged the tchotchkes on the gift shelves. "I have no idea what couples do—I'm here on the weekend with groups of women. I can't recall the last time I saw a couple."

Next to the front door stood a pine writing desk with a phone, a reservation book, and an answering machine. Reaching out, Margaret pushed the blinking red message button.

"Hey, it's Lauren, I'm gonna be late. I got an audition at ten," said a careless, cigarette-sucking voice.

"I must stop hiring actresses," Margaret muttered.

"You've got to stick with the older ones that never work," said Lilly.

There was a sharp bang at the back door, followed by a gust of cool air and, finally, Clarissa Richardson. Beautiful and just a gasp from forty, she favored theatrical attire and Bakelite bracelets.

Without so much as a hello, she breezed in with the day's dilemma.

"My cell is almost dead and my agent's supposed to call!" Rummaging through her bulging purse, she spilled a pair of eyeglasses on the floor.

Lilly playfully scooped up the emerald-green frames

and dangled them in her face. "When did you start wearing these?"

Clarissa snatched them back. "They're for driving."

"Uh-oh! Can estrogen replacement be far behind?"

"What are you talking about? I'm still in my thirties."

Is that in dog years? Lilly thought.

"I suppose you've already prepped the sandwiches so we don't have to wait like yesterday." Clarissa looked pointedly at Margaret.

Deciding to separate the two, Margaret made a preemptive strike. "Lilly," she said smoothly, giving her chef a little push towards the kitchen. "Please finish up with the scones."

Lilly swiveled on her heel and trudged back down the hall.

"Five minutes is not a wait!" she shot back.

Margaret paused until Lilly was out of earshot, then whispered, "Was there a problem yesterday?"

Lowering her chin, Clarissa clasped her hand to her throat to underscore the graveness of the situation. "After you left for your teeth cleaning, she forgot to put the leaves in the teapot and then she forgot to boil the eggs for the egg salad."

"I see," Margaret said thoughtfully. "Clarissa, please check the rest of the messages before you make your call. And do hurry. Lauren's going to be late."

"Did her nose ring get infected?"

"An audition. Thank god I can count on you."

"I go on auditions!"

"I meant that as a compliment," Margaret said.

Clarissa's green eyes burned brightly. "I might have an audition later. A killer part. Just perfect for me."

Back in the kitchen, Margaret kept a watchful eye on her chef. She knew there was truth in what Clarissa had said. Lilly *had* been very absentminded lately. Last week some of the customers had complained about the scones. They were metallic tasting, probably a result of too much baking soda. Margaret shuddered. That was the trouble with running your own business, she thought. You could never really let up. Otherwise, you had inedible, horrid scones.

Settled at the writing desk, Clarissa ignored the answering machine and, instead, reached for the land line. She dialed her agent, or rather, her agent's assistant, since she rarely spoke directly to him these days. "Amy? It's Clarissa Richardson again. Is Ken in yet? I have to get into that pilot, *Lavender and Lace*. I'm perfect for the part of Scarlett Finnegan."

"I think that role's for twenty-five to thirty," replied Amy in a dismissive tone cultivated by young agents-in-training.

"No, it's thirty to thirty-five. I saw the break-downs." Where does he find these girls? she thought angrily. They know nothing about acting except acting like they know everything.

"I'll give Ken *all* your messages." Amy hung up the phone.

Remember my extensive range, Clarissa prayed silently. Then, closing her eyes, she repeated her affirmations. *I am an extraordinarily good actress. I love myself and I am will-ing to have success in my life.*

Lilly tossed cubes of cold, unsalted butter and four cups of flour into the food processor. Then she hit the pulse button. When was Clarissa going to get it? she thought. It didn't matter how great she was as an actor or how hard she worked. Success so often depended on those other, intangible things. Things like who you know and who you meet.

And how lucky you were.

Unlocking the lid of the machine, she reached into the bowl and rubbed her fingers through the flour. It felt like coarse cornmeal—perfect. Dumping the mix into a large stainless steel bowl, she added buttermilk and stirred until the batter came together.

Turning the dough out onto the wooden counter, she began to pat it into two smooth circles. She remembered how her mother, Cora, would often keep her up at night, crying about the parts she didn't get. The two of them had lived on canned beans and Birds Eye frozen vegetables for several years until Cora finally landed a soap.

A part she got because the producer's first choice came down with pneumonia. And the thing that will keep you off a soap is sickness. You had to be there five days a week for forty-eight weeks a year.

With a chef's knife, Lilly cut each round into six triangles. She beat an egg with a little milk, then brushed the wash over the scones. Clarissa's a better actress than my mother was, she thought. But Cora was lucky. She was in the right place at the right time plus she had me for the emotional support. Clarissa has no one. No daughter to cook for her, clean for her, listen to her nervous breakdowns.

Lilly felt a little guilty for riding Clarissa so hard. Acting wasn't something you picked; it was in your genes. Like brown eyes or schizophrenia.

Placing her scones on a parchment-lined baking sheet, she popped them in the oven.

While watching her cell phone for signs of life, Clarissa listened to the phone machine. A woman with a heavy English accent had just started speaking when the cell buzzed. She checked the caller ID.

Ken!

Stopping the machine, she frantically opened her phone. "Hello?"

"Liss," her agent cooed, "we need to talk."

Something in his tone set her on edge and she braced herself against the top of the desk. "Ken, I know that Amy is new and she doesn't know my range but—"

"Liss, we're doing a lot of reorganizing around here. Sort of defining our mission statement and who and what applies to that goal."

"What?" Her phone began the beep, beep of low power.

"Liss, you know I love you but frankly, I'm not seeing work that's right for you and I'm not sure our synergy is creating opportunity."

"What?" Preoccupied with her battery, she didn't catch what he was saying.

He paused. "Listen, I think right now you'd be better off with someone who could give you the attention you deserve."

Beads of sweat broke out on her upper lip. "Ken, I've been with you almost twenty years."

"Exactly. Exactly! I'm glad we're on the same page. Change is difficult, but really, it's for the best. And of course, we'll always be friends . . . we'll still see each other, oh, who is it, Amy?"

Clarissa wondered if she were levitating. "Ken, we have to discuss this in person!"

"Can't, I've got to take this other call. Don't view this as a negative . . ."

Her phone died. He was gone.

Now Ken and that hateful Amy were not even a thorn in her side.

Too late, Clarissa realized that a lousy agent was better than nothing at all.

Chapter Two

~ ~

Dueling police sirens on La Brea forced Lauren from her dreamy morning sleep. Opening her eyes, she saw Dakota. White and chiseled like those gorgeous Italian statues, he had blond curly hair that was always rumpled in the sexiest way. His fingertips and toes and penis were rosy patches on an otherwise milky frame.

She kissed him. "What time is it?"

He fished around on the floor for his cell phone. "Ten."

"Fuck!"

"Let's."

"Can't. I've got work."

Lauren shimmied into low-cut jeans and the flimsiest spaghetti-strap camisole. At twenty-six, a night of drinking, sex, and little sleep only enhanced her looks.

"Don't leave," he reached for the remote and clicked on *Comedy Central*.

"I've got a day job."

"I'll support us."

Lauren rolled her tawny cat eyes. Dakota could live on nothing. He worked part time in tech support to finance his real mission—creating his own awesome computer game.

"What do you need?" he smiled lazily and pulled her back to bed.

"Oh, everything," she murmured. God he was cute! If she didn't shower, go back to her place, or stop for coffee, there was time for one more round before work.

The tearoom was filling up when Lauren crept in the back door.

"Sorry I'm late," she said, peeling off a cropped velvet jacket suitable for dim lights and a cash bar.

Margaret, who was steeping two pots of tea, jerked around and took in the scanty top and nose jewelry.

"Did you get my message?" Lauren said, "I—"

"Please remove that ring." Margaret was pissed in that quiet English way. Her mouth was pursed. Lauren quickly unclasped the offending silver hoop from her right nostril and shoved it in the pocket of her jeans.

"Can I borrow the white shirt?" said Lauren, pointing at the hook on the wall. "Because of my . . . audition this morning, I forgot my other clothes."

"Fine," Margaret nodded. She always kept something at the ready for these types of emergencies.

Lauren buttoned herself up and then tied on a Scotch-plaid apron. She glanced at Margaret shyly. "Will you put up my hair like you did last week?"

"If you'd like."

"I had no idea we were going to play beauty parlor," Lilly said, shoving another tray of scones into the oven.

From the drawer under the wall phone, Margaret retrieved some bobby pins and twisted Lauren's feathery strands into a smooth chignon.

"There, you look lovely," she said, standing back to admire her work. A timer buzzed and she returned to her teapots, fishing out the mesh balls stuffed with soggy leaves. She handed Lauren the Earl Grey. "Go on, now. This is for the sisters by the window."

Feeling elegant in her upswept do, Lauren slipped gracefully through the doorway.

Lilly looked sharply at her boss. "You know she's an operator."

"Yes, an awfully good one," said Margaret, setting up a silver tray with four cups. "But she's quite pretty. People like to look at her. Such a pity she dresses like a two-bit tart. When I was her age, we wanted to look beautiful."

"Everyone that age is beautiful," said Lilly.

Margaret whisked the pot of English Breakfast to the Book Club, who, judging by the copies of *Jane and Prudence* on the table, had chosen Barbara Pym for this month's discussion. Pouring out their steaming brew, she murmured, "Such a witty book," while struggling to recall if Tony had ever told her she was pretty.

No. But he had often said that she was brilliant and chic.

Oh, dear, Margaret thought sadly. I should have known then.

Lilly was beating chocolate ganache and Clarissa was arranging sandwiches on a silver caddy when Lauren returned for her customers' scones.

"You're welcome," Clarissa said rudely.

"For what?" Lauren stuck her finger in Lilly's bowl of chocolate and began lapping it up.

"Once again you were late so I had to cover for you." Clarissa grasped the handle of her caddy and swept from the room.

She's just jealous, Lauren thought, dropping two scones on two small plates. She probably hasn't been laid in a year.

"You look good with your hair up," said Lilly, all the while thinking, *Fuck, she is hot!*

"Hey, Lil, would you make me some espresso? I never got my coffee this morning."

"Sure." While grinding the coffee beans, Lilly fantasized about ripping that shirt off Lauren's bikini-perfect body. "So, who're you seeing this week?"

"This computer guy, Dakota. He's cute but kinda laid-back."

"You say that like it's a bad thing."

"He doesn't seem to care that much about money."

"He's what? Twenty-five?"

"He should be more ambitious."

Lilly tamped the grounds down in the filter basket. "When I was twenty-five I thought if I was in love and getting laid it was ambitious."

"You still think that way."

Lilly went home to a dark house that night. Deborah had a meeting. It was pilot season and the network executives were working fourteen-hour days making shows that no one would ever see.

This business, she thought, it's a life sentence.

She lit all the lamps in the living room, stuck Laura Nyro in the CD player, and sat down on the sofa to roll a joint. She couldn't believe she was living with a casting director, although it was a step up from her last two girlfriends. At least Deborah was employed. Melanie, a video artist, had spent her days smoking cigarettes with friends at coffeehouses and Carla, a set dresser, had injured her back and required enormous sums of Lilly's money for a chiropractor and aromatherapy.

Lilly hated to be home alone. It reminded her of childhood, spending her afternoons with cinnamon toast and the television as companions. She and Cora lived in Westwood, in a Spanish duplex behind a wrought-iron gate and a small courtyard with an empty fishpond. Cora had played the faithful nurse Rosie on *Mass General* for twenty years until lung cancer took her at fifty. The age I am now, Lilly thought, inhaling the sweet high. But I don't have a daughter—no, I mean an indentured servant—to wait on me.

Lying back on the blue cotton cushions, she pushed

Cora out of her mind. No sense in wasting a perfectly good high on that relationship. She thought, instead, about meeting Deborah at the Silver Lake dog park. Lilly didn't own a dog, but she went there to hang out with all the cute women and their Australian shepherds and Labradors.

A tiny freckle-faced brunette was wrangling a pair of beagles. The dogs howled and whined but Lilly didn't hear them over the din of her lust. She wanted Deborah so badly she pretended to admire the annoying beasts that brought them together.

Fresh from New York, Deborah was working as a dog walker but searching for a job in entertainment. Lilly used her gal pals to arrange an interview for Deb at a top-rated network. Assistant to Vice-President of Casting. That was three years ago. Now Deb was a VP herself.

So she was never home.

Lilly cooked for them, cleaned for them, and took Deborah's gorgeous stretch wool jackets to the dry cleaner.

I guess that makes me her assistant, Lilly mused.

Deb didn't want so much sex anymore. The power at work was the juice.

And I'm fat, Lilly thought. If I could give up the pot, I'd lose thirty pounds.

But what would I do if I wasn't smoking the pot?

Chapter Three

Clarissa knocked on Mark's door. He was supposed to be home by now. They had to work
on their scene before class tonight.

Fucking actors, she thought.

Dropping into a padded teak chair on the porch, she took
in the view of the basin. Vermont Avenue and Western Avenue were twinkling on the north/south grid. Century City
was dimly visible in the waning winter light. This was prime
real estate courtesy of beer commercials. Mark had landed a
national campaign and the house and car followed.

I never book commercial jobs, she thought bitterly. You
had to have a certain look. Or maybe it was the willingness
to shamelessly pitch the virtues of vile, useless things that
people didn't need. Anyway, she was too serious, too dramatic for advertising.

Mark said he wanted to be a legitimate actor. But he wanted to pursue it from the lap of luxury.

His sleek European sedan pulled into the driveway. Blessed with curly hair and a sublimely square jaw, Mark eased himself out of the tan leather seat.

"Sorry, Liss, my trainer was late."

Inside the house, envy threatened to suffocate her. Mid-century pieces mixed perfectly with Baroque velvet drapes and a Warhol print. Even if she made a million dollars she'd never have taste this good.

Just focus on the work, she told herself sternly. Their scene was about loss and hope—two themes Clarissa was very familiar with—and when she started reading, the tea-room, her agent, the pain over not having Mark's money, melted away.

It was the dialogue and the way she slipped into another skin. This was it for her. Acting fed her soul more than material things ever would.

Why couldn't she make it pay?

Later in class, when they played the scene, she felt the power of capturing her audience. For a few minutes in the darkened theater, she reached out and, with her magical acting skills, she made them fall in love with her.

"You were amazing," Mark said afterwards, gathering up his water bottle and phone. "You're so good at this."

I've always been good at this, Clarissa thought.

Vince DeFaria, their acting coach, put a hand on Mark's shoulder.

"Great work," he said, looking directly at Clarissa.

"I really felt I connected," said Mark, smiling coyly at Vince.

Doesn't he know Vince is straight? Clarissa wondered. With that gorgeous voice and a face to match, she was sure Vince had plenty of women to choose from. Besides, he had the whole acting coach guru thing that assured a steady supply of sex.

Thank god I never date actors, she thought. Guaranteed heartache.

The last of the students drifted away when they realized that Mark had claimed Vince and wasn't going to share. "I've learned so much in your class," Mark was gushing to his coach. "When I was in high school, I was always, like, Second Serf on the Left."

Vince laughed and his easy grin made him look younger than his probably forty years. His intense brown eyes gazed down at Clarissa. "I bet you were always the lead."

"It's true," she said. "I was Juliet and Laura and Ophelia."

"Where was this?" said Vince, crushing Mark's hopes for further attention.

"Topsfield High. In Massachusetts. I was the queen of drama class."

"Weren't we all," said Mark dryly.

"People always said I'd go far," she said, immediately regretting her remark.

She hadn't gone far. She still wasn't there.

"I'm sorry . . . I have to go," she said abruptly. Vince

looked surprised. She wondered what it'd be like to kiss that mouth.

Driving back home to Laurel Canyon, she listened to her voicemail. Bill had called and said he couldn't come over because of his kid.

Annoyed, she tossed the phone on the passenger seat. Great! Her evening was ruined. The triumph of tonight's performance receded under the weight of loneliness and failure. When she got home, she took a Tylenol PM, climbed into bed, and pulled down her sleep mask. She added a caveat to her imaginary rulebook: No more married men. They came too soon or they didn't come at all.

Listening to the distant hum of traffic on Laurel Canyon she wondered if Vince ever dated his students. He seemed so professional. But she knew better. There wasn't an acting teacher alive that didn't sleep with his adoring disciples. And she didn't want to be just another lay.

Acting is my temple, she thought sleepily, I must keep it sacred.

The following day at Magpie's, Clarissa had passed through shock into raw panic. "How will I work without an agent?" she said to Margaret and Lilly, nervously cutting the cucumber sandwiches for the four o'clock wedding shower.

"You don't need an agent to audition. You know casting directors and producers." Margaret cringed at Clarissa's handiwork. The sandwiches looked like they'd been shredded with cuticle scissors.

"What will I say when people ask me who my agent is?"

"Tell them you're still with Ken," Lilly said. "If you get the job he'll take you back for the ten percent." She recut the triangles and stacked them onto a doily-lined tea caddy.

Clarissa shivered. "But he said it's over. He hasn't gotten me a job in months."

"That liar. You haven't worked in two years," Lilly shot back.

Margaret, aware that this conversation would only lead to self-loathing, stuck the caddy into Clarissa's hands and directed her towards the tearoom.

The bridal shower oohed and ahhed over the tower of precious sandwiches. Clarissa thought the bride-to-be looked awfully familiar. A blonde in her early forties, she appeared months younger from the injections.

Blonde Botox spied the creamy yellow spread peeking out between several of the white triangles.

"No one does egg." She looked accusingly at Clarissa.

"There's also cucumber, watercress, and French ham sandwiches," Clarissa replied.

"Take them back and bring us more cucumber," Botox said.

Clarissa delivered the caddy back to the kitchen.

"The bitches don't eat egg."

Lilly frowned. "We're getting a lot of that lately." She heaped the offending sandwiches on a plate and, with a deep sigh, began to slice up more cucumber.

Clarissa resumed her personal life. "What am I going to do? Acting is deep in my soul, it's the core of my being . . . it's my life!"

And that's pathetic, thought Lilly.

"If I don't get that audition, I'm giving up acting forever." Clarissa threw back her shoulders as if waiting for the curtain to fall.

"No actress voluntarily gives up acting," said Lilly. "You have to be forced out: pregnancy, insanity . . . a felony conviction."

Clarissa returned to the shower with fresh sandwiches. Suddenly she recognized Botox: she'd been a guest star on *Detective Buck Love* fifteen years ago. She had played a love interest poisoned by a drug dealer seeking revenge against Buck. They killed her off because she was such a bad actress.

But now she sported a HUGE diamond ring.

God, I hope she doesn't remember me, Clarissa prayed.

"Didn't you used to be on *Detective Buck Love*?" Botox smiled, baring her teeth. "I think we worked together."

"Oh, yeah," Clarissa said weakly, "I thought you looked familiar."

Botox gushed to her tablemates. "I *guest starred* on that show!"

"Wow," someone murmured. "That was a really big series."

"I was the female lead!" All eyes turned quickly to Clarissa, then back to Botox for her reaction.

Botox's eyes narrowed. "Then why are you working here?"

Clarissa burned with shame. Why had she let her pride out of the tamperproof safe?

You were only as good as your last show. And *Detective Buck Love* was canceled fourteen years ago.

"I'm here because it's important to carry on the tea tradition," Clarissa said, repeating one of Margaret's favorite tenets. "We all need a respite from the hectic pace of modern life."

"We do!" agreed the ladies of the tea party.

Shooting a dismissive glance at Clarissa, Botox moved on to her mountain of presents.

With the bearing of a queen, Clarissa made her exit.

I'd say that was a rather good imitation of me, thought Margaret approvingly. She had watched the entire performance from her desk by the front door. She remembered back a couple of years ago, when she and Lilly had gone down to the Old Globe to see Clarissa in *Taming of the Shrew*. Her Kate had been brilliant.

Adding up the day's receipts, Margaret wondered why it was that happily engaged women felt the need to be cruel to their less fortunate sisters.

Could it be that acting trumped happiness?

Driving home that night, Margaret bailed from La Cienega, which was down to one lane and at a complete standstill. Zigzagging through residential side streets, she suddenly realized she was on her old block. There was the house she and Tony rented when they first arrived. Impulsively, she pulled over.

My god, she thought, I barely recognize it. Once upon a time it had been a cute Mediterranean stucco. Now it sported three stories, two balconies, shutters, palm trees, and maroon-striped awnings.

When we lived there, it was small and charming. And we were happy.

With the warm weather and their very own orange trees, the Moores had found themselves in paradise. Tony was starring in *Hair* and they were always going round to drinks parties and dinners. He landed quite a few jobs from people he met over pasta primavera and Chardonnay.

At a certain point, they simply had to reciprocate. Booze was expensive and neither of them could manage a three-course dinner. But Margaret could make sandwiches and had a flair for arranging them beautifully on the table. She had the recipe for her grandmother's scones and a source for Devon cream, which was hard to find back then. They had a lush lawn in the back where they set up croquet—an enormous hit with Americans. Sunday afternoon tea at The Moores became a sought-after invitation.

Then, after a decade and a great deal of drinking, Tony's star had faded. With a little money and his knack for antiquing, Margaret opened up what she thought every woman wanted: an English tearoom, not too fancy, very comfortable, and most of all, reliable. A place you could count on for bridal showers, birthdays, or a stolen afternoon with a dear friend.

Pulling away from the curb Margaret thought it had been sweet back then. But if anyone had told her, thirty years ago, that she'd still be living in Los Angeles, she'd never have believed them.

Chapter Four

Off a busy street in Hollywood, below a blue neon sign that softly glowed "Two Thousand," there was a plain metal door. Lauren pushed it open and clomped down a dim corridor with stark arrangements of rocks, candles, and water. Making a left at a goldleaf Buddha, she reached a reflecting pool with floating lotus blossoms. Standing behind a mahogany lectern was a hostess checking names, but really, just checking her style passport. The music was the sort of frenetic beat that could trigger a heart attack or an orgasm, depending on your state of mind. Or your date for the evening.

Lauren was alone, but she was meeting People.

They were nestled behind saffron curtains in a cushioned and sequined dining pit. She pounced on the short guy with hipster glasses, jeans, and a paisley shirt.

She could spy SUCCESSFUL in a nanosecond. Just look for the opposite of Lakeland, Florida, and there it is.

With thinning hair and a graying complexion, Andy was a young producer who just looked old. Tossing back her silvery tresses, Lauren presented her full and flirty breasts, beautifully displayed in a lace bra and persimmon-colored babydoll dress.

Andy ordered her a Champagne cocktail and she nudged his thigh with her knee. What had he produced? she asked. I love that show. She was breathy and adorable and wet.

Now this was acting.

They left the club and she followed his silver BMW up Cahuenga towards the Hollywood Reservoir. An enormous cement and steel box, his house resembled an ocean liner that had somehow crashed into the hillside and would eventually sink to the bottom of the canyon below.

Once inside the bedroom, Lauren couldn't wait to take her clothes off. The lust in Andy's eyes when he saw her naked was thrilling. Boys always went for her big time. That's why her mom told her to move to LA. Boys there will love you, too, Vicky said. And they'll be rich. Plus there's no alligators and no humidity like Florida.

Fortunately, she'd had two drinks, which helped to transform their perfectly mediocre sex into something a bit more wild and loose. Andy seemed lost in unfamiliar territory when he went down on her but it was okay. For Lauren, the most important thing was to be desired.

They fell asleep against his blue flannel sheets with the hum of an air purifier in the background.

About three AM the alcohol wore off and her eyes flew open. Quietly lifting a cashmere throw from the foot of the bed, she wrapped it around her and, grabbing her phone, tiptoed out the door.

She was fascinated with Andy's house and Andy's things. Touring the rooms, she enjoyed being alone with the leather reading chair, the framed movie posters, and the dining room table piled with scripts. She knew, somehow, that everything was expensive. It reminded her of a museum; it wasn't like any place back in Florida.

She drifted into his immaculate slate kitchen. Like so many men with state-of-the-art appliances, Andy didn't cook.

She dialed Dakota. He answered on the first ring.

"What 'cha doing?" she said.

"Working." The tragic wail of Kurt Cobain was bleating in the background. "Wanna come over?"

"Not tonight."

"Tomorrow?"

"Okay."

She hung up happily. She was never more satisfied than when two men wanted her.

Sneaking into the bathroom, she assessed the medicine cabinet: Rogaine, Advil, and Ambien.

Popping an Ambien, she slipped back into bed, taking care not to bump Andy's flaccid rear end.

In the morning they went to Starbucks and while he talked on the phone, Lauren sucked on a caramel frappuccino and wondered why so many successful guys were awkward in bed. Then she fantasized about Dakota and his beautiful tapered fingers.

"That was Glori, the casting director of *Lavender*," Andy said, interrupting her sex dream. "I got you an audition."

"Really?" She threw her arms around his weak shoulders.

Driving back to her place she changed her mind about Andy. In the daylight, sipping espresso and working a cell phone, he was pretty sexy after all.

By seven AM that same morning, Deborah had already logged three miles on her treadmill. It was set up next to the living room window, so she had a great view of the Silver Lake Reservoir and the people running around it. She showered, then chose an ivory blouse with a cascading ruffle and slightly flared taupe pants—power suits were out, feminine style was in. Then she carried her laptop into the kitchen and sat down at the table.

Lilly, in a flannel robe and chef's clogs, pulled a Dutch apple pancake out of the oven. It was light, puffy, and magnificent.

"Forget it," snapped Deborah, dismissing the pastry. "You know I'm not doing carbs."

"You're in shape for the two of us," said Lilly, dusting the golden crust with powdered sugar. "You're someone who could actually eat this without dire consequences."

"Stop the sabotage," said Deborah. She was skimming the paper, checking email, and cradling her cell.

"Can we have breakfast without the office?" Lilly sighed. "I'd like to talk. You gulp, scan, and split."

Deborah snapped off the toys. "Okay, but I'm only doing fruit and maybe an egg white."

Lilly set a pan on the stove to boil. She had perfected the soft-boiled egg—six minutes timed from first entry into simmering water. People loved her eggs.

"Let's go away this weekend," Lilly smiled. "It's my Saturday off from the tearoom."

"Lilly—pilot season."

"Two days! There's a B&B in Mammoth I want to check out . . . right on Lake George. Great snowshoeing. You'd like that."

"Go without me." Deborah disappeared into the paper. "You know I hate those places. Wine and cheese with old people, ick."

How old are old people? Lilly worried.

When the timer rang, she carried the pot to the sink and ran cold water over the eggs. She tapped their shells with a spoon and teased the slippery white ovals out into a small bowl. With a dash of pepper, they were really the perfect food.

"Have you heard of *Lavender and Lace*?" she said, presenting the eggs to Deborah.

"Yeah . . . pedestrian soap. Why are you suddenly interested in pilots?" Deborah's eyes gleamed. Business talk turned her on. I should probably read *Variety* to her for foreplay, Lilly thought.

"Clarissa wants a part in it."

"Is she any good?" wondered Deborah between bites of egg white and glances at the Calendar section.

"Yeah. That's what makes it so tragic."

"Who's her agent?"

"Ken Shapiro."

"Never heard of him." Deborah collected her gear. "I've got an eight-thirty breakfast meeting."

"You'll eat someone else's breakfast?" Lilly was dismayed.

"No one eats at breakfast meetings."

"Do you hear yourself?"

Deborah kissed her and left.

Lilly was appalled at the food issues in this town. The denizens treated their sustenance with suspicion, like a mortal enemy. Wheat triggered allergies, milk harbored pesticides, fish carried toxins, and sugar—the holy grail of food hysteria—was addictive and the root of ADHD. We are a nation of ninnies, Lilly thought.

But not me.

She bussed her plate into the living room and settled down on the sofa. Picking up the remote, she clicked on the morning news show and tucked heartily into the apple pancake.

Dragging herself into Magpie's that morning, Lauren hopped up on the counter and watched Lilly pinch dough into small metal tart pans.

Fuck this place, she thought, lighting up a cigarette.

I should be in spinning class. I have to look good for that audition.

Lilly opened the window to let out the smoke. "You know Margaret forbids that."

"She's not my mother."

She should have been, Lilly thought.

"Guess what? I've got an audition tomorrow. Some pilot. *Lavender and Lady* or something."

Lilly froze. Don't get involved! she told herself.

"This guy I met is the producer."

"That guy you're seeing?" said Lilly.

"Nah, the guy I'm fucking," said Lauren, yawning.

"Your generation is so romantic."

Lauren smiled coyly. "Make me espresso?"

"Not right now," said Lilly. "Produce is late so I've got to get everything else finished before it gets here."

Clarissa entered and saw Lauren's cigarette. "Why do you defy Margaret? She's so nice to you."

"So?"

"Besides, smoking gives you wrinkles," said Clarissa.

"Then you'd better not smoke." Lauren stuck the butt in her mouth and, raking her fingers through her hair, twisted the strands into a sloppy chignon.

Clarissa stole a look at her own reflection in a silver platter. Luckily, she had great genes. Her mother's skin was practically flawless and she never, ever, went out in the sun.

"Fred's Finest!" A trim Latina carried in a crate of mangoes and heaved them onto the kitchen counter. A thick brunette ponytail jutted out from behind her kelly-green baseball cap. Appraising the group, she approached the chef's jacket. "I'm Stephanie, your new produce coordinator," she said, pumping Lilly's sticky hand.

Lilly frowned. "Where's Larry?"

"He got a series."

"The one about the aliens or the personal trainers?" Lilly puzzled over the tropical fruit in Stephanie's crate.

"I think the trainers."

"Men have got it made," said Clarissa, heading outside to work her phone. "Larry is at least forty-two, he's going bald, and still, they cast him as a personal trainer?"

Lilly scanned the packing slip. "This is for Teaser's not Tearoom."

Stephanie frowned. "Are you sure? I don't have nothing else on the truck . . . this is my last stop."

Lilly glanced at the clock: ten-thirty. Nothing was prepped. Customers in an hour.

Margaret arrived and immediately smelled the burning cigarette. Before she could lecture, Lauren jumped off the counter and dashed outside. Then Margaret noticed Stephanie. "Where's Larry?"

"He got a series."

"The aliens?"

"Personal trainers."

Margaret surveyed the crate. "That is not our produce."

"The warehouse made a mistake but I'll fix it," Stephanie said. "I'll be back in twenty minutes."

"It takes twenty to get downtown!" Lilly said.

"It takes forty—with no traffic," Margaret said. "I'm calling Big Fred. This is the third mixup this month!"

Stephanie's confident demeanor began to crack. "Big Fred's in rehab!"

"When's he going to get his shit together?" said Lilly.

Margaret reached for the wall phone. "I am sympathetic to his ongoing travails," she said to the pretty produce coordinator, "but my dear, I have a business to run."

Stephanie's large brown eyes grew bright. "Please, lady! Freddy Jr.'s in charge now! If he finds I messed up, he'll send me back to the loading dock. Man, that place is cold and dark and the guys there . . . you don't wanna know . . ."

Margaret held up her right hand. "Please compose yourself." Stephanie clamped her mouth shut.

There was a moment of silence while Margaret gazed at the clock. Finally, she turned back to Stephanie. "We all know it takes forty-five minutes—minimum!—to get anywhere in LA. So this is what we're going to do. You are going to give me three days' credit and I'm going to the market down the street and buy the produce myself at retail prices."

"But it'll come out of my paycheck!"

"That's between you and Fred Jr."

Stephanie rubbed her eyes with her shirtsleeve. "Okay. My career goal is to be a number one coordinator."

The kitchen jammed. Lilly filled the baked tart shells with lemon curd and whipped cream. Clarissa cut sandwich bread and spooned jam into dainty china bowls. Tables were set. Flowers were primped. Margaret returned with the produce and they all assembled cucumber and watercress sandwiches, which they then covered with damp cheese-cloth to keep them fresh. They worked quietly, lost in their own thoughts, and the routine was comforting.

Margaret switched on the fire next to the coveted prize table. They were fully booked today so they'd be running. They took a bit of respite in the preparations.

The Goldstein-Sutton baby shower arrived: an upscale lesbian couple in their early thirties plus forty professional friends. They claimed the room with their gigantic leather totes, their presents, and their phones.

Lauren sidled up to Lilly in the kitchen.

"I am NEVER having a baby. That woman is six feet wide."

"I can't really see you as a mother—unless you were accidentally impregnated by an alien."

"I go out on auditions for mothers."

"That's because TV mothers are fifteen years younger than real life ones," said Clarissa, bringing in an empty tea-pot. "Even if the character has five kids she's supposed to look like she's never been pregnant."

Feeling curious about these mothers-to-be, Lilly left her kitchen outpost and, standing at the doorway, peeked in at the expectant parents. One was dark and slim in a severe black jacket, the other beet faced and hugely pregnant. They were smiling happily at an enormous baby stroller with double cup holders.

I hate them, Lilly thought.

Pretending to check on the food, she casually entered the room and surveyed the table laden with the unwrapped booty. There were cotton jammies, a baby activity blanket, and a tiny pair of sneakers. Picking up a porcelain bowl featuring Peter Rabbit, she felt a quickening in her chest.

"Can you believe all this stuff?" said the dark slim mom, heaving a Pima cotton comforter on the expanding pile.

"I guess babies need . . . their own china?" Lilly said, quickly putting down Peter Rabbit.

"It's sort of nauseating," said Slim, taking a slightly militant tone. "I mean, is it progress when lesbians are as greedy as the straights?"

"Hey, twenty years ago, we never dreamed we'd get to be married, let alone become mothers." Lilly was irritated. This gal had no idea how it used to be. What an entitled breeder.

Slim studied Lilly, who was stroking a plush brown bear. "It's still not too late," she said kindly. "There's a world of fertility out there."

Not for me, thought Lilly. Deborah doesn't want a baby and neither did Melanie. Carla—please!—she was the baby! No, I'm always in the wrong place in time and usually with the wrong person.

Gently returning Mr. Bear to the table, she smiled weakly at Slim. "Have you got enough scones?"

When the last customers relinquished their teacups and headed home to their families, Lilly began to clean up. She decided to take the time to set her *mise en place* in order. No sense in hurrying back to an empty house.

Loading the dishwasher she admitted to herself the other, deeper reason for not pushing for a baby: she was afraid to go back to childhood again. Maybe one childhood per lifetime is enough for people like me. Wiping down the counters she suddenly flashed on Mr. Klinefelter's kitchen and the bold black and yellow tiles. He had once been their upstairs tenant. Cora—although a total mess in her personal life—had always been wise about money. The minute she'd landed a steady gig, she'd bought the duplex and rented out the other unit.

Mr. Klinefelter was a retired German teacher who loved cooking and the opera. He and Lilly would sometimes watch Julia Child and then attempt to re-create the dishes. Together they mastered veal cordon bleu and beurre blanc sauce. They rolled up their sleeves and kneaded and pounded dough. While it rested, Mr. Klinefelter would recap the plot of *La Bohème* or instruct her on the Teutonic origins of English words. Sometimes he'd reminisce about his dead wife, Elsie, who, he said, made the best apple strudel in the world.

Cora was a vampire. She'd get home from work at five and pour herself a drink. She'd be sauced by seven, so Lilly fed herself. If it had been up to Cora, she would have lived on crackers, cheese, and Chablis. Until Mr. Klinefelter taught her how to broil chops and bake potatoes, Lilly ate Swanson's TV Dinners. Lilly was grateful to him for the cooking.

Cora's alcoholic slumber usually wore off around eleven PM when she would stumble into Lilly's room and sit on the bed.

"Help me with my lines," she'd beg.

The line reading took twenty minutes. The monologue about men, her career, her loneliness . . . that took another two hours.

Around one AM Cora would finally pass out and Lilly could go back to sleep.

Lilly kept to herself at school—who would want to bring friends home to Vampira?—so Mr. Klinefelter was her only real friend. I wonder if he ever knew about Cora, about us? she thought with shame, hanging her utensils on the overhead metal rack. He never said anything. Well, really, what could he say? Back then no one talked about child abuse or neglect. You just muddled through and did the best you could. There was no therapy. There was just . . . cooking and eventual escape.

At seventeen, Lilly moved out to a crappy apartment in Hollywood. She took a job with a caterer and found excuses not to visit her mother.

But when Cora was dying, Lilly returned home and took care of her. One afternoon, sitting side by side on Cora's bed, mother and daughter discussed the funeral arrangements.

"I want music—'Moon River,'" Cora said, "and I want to be buried in Westwood Memorial Park with all the classy people."

Lilly discovered that the cemetery was mega expensive and they couldn't afford a plot.

"But your ashes could stay there, for eternity, in the vault," Lilly told her.

Cora insisted they visit. So Lilly pushed her mother's wheelchair around the circular drive to the quiet, austere building that held the tasteful urns of the well to do.

"This is actually better," Cora said, nodding her approval. "From here I'm closer to Marilyn Monroe."

God, is that the best we can hope for? Lilly frowned, as she folded up her dish towels and clicked off the kitchen light. That when it's all over, you'll rest in eternity next to another totally depressing alcoholic actress?

No, she decided emphatically, as she set the security alarm and shut the back door. When it's all over I want my ashes thrown on a compost pile.

I want to rest, in eternity, in the rich soil of mother earth . . . then hopefully return as a blazing, red tomato.

Chapter Five

*quashing the mayo into the egg yolks, Margaret was bored. Slicing the cucumber, Margaret was bored.

I've been on 3rd Street for twenty bloody years, she thought. Today it feels like fifty.

"You're turning that into soup," Lilly said, interrupting Margaret's silent bitching.

"You're right, here . . ." Margaret handed Lilly the bowl of egg salad. "Today is one of those days."

"Oh," said Lilly. "When the sight of dainty sandwiches makes you sick?"

"Yes, I suppose so."

"If you didn't own a tearoom, what would you do?"

"Let's not get carried away," Margaret shuddered. Americans were always so eager to reinvent themselves. An

Englishwoman doesn't start over at fifty-six. It's not in our genes. We stay the course.

"Oh, let's get carried away," said Lilly, "just for fun. If you could do something different, anything at all, what would it be?"

Margaret thought for a moment. "I expect I'd sell my house and leave the city."

"And go where?"

"Back to England."

"London?"

"I don't think I could afford London now." Margaret thought about rolling grassy hills and cows. She smiled. "The country."

"What does one do in the country?" said Lilly, in her best *Masterpiece Theatre* accent.

"Take long walks. Visit my neighbors. Join a parish, I suppose."

Lilly arched her eyebrows. "Since when do you go to church?"

"It's the Church of England," Margaret said by way of explanation.

"You'd probably garden."

"Now that Kate is grown I don't intend to raise anything, ever again."

"Well then," said Lilly, "after a walk and a chat with neighbors . . . what would you do with the next twelve hours in a day?"

Once tempted to consider the possibility of change, Margaret found she couldn't stop.

"It's funny," she said to Lilly as they closed the shop and headed up the street to dinner. "I came here because of Tony, and I stayed because of Kate and I'm not sure I ever charted my course in life."

"Who charts their own course?" said Lilly. "It's all a crapshoot. We're all drifting . . . only sometimes we luck out and bump into something good."

They stared into a fashionably bleak store window. "Remember when this block was nothing but shoe repair and junky antiques shops?" said Lilly.

"Let's go inside," said Margaret, eager to drop this conversation about the general letdown of life.

The boutique had gray walls, a cement floor, and an enormous crystal chandelier. There appeared to be only six dresses hanging from six stainless steel trapeze bars.

Lilly tugged the sleeve of a black jersey dress and gasped at the price tag, "Two thousand dollars!"

They left the shop and strolled past a rare books store, its window cluttered with aged volumes, antique maps, and a spinning globe (Wonderful, important, enriches the community, Margaret thought approvingly), then a scented candle emporium ("What the hell does Black Cherry Rain smell like?" said Lilly) and finally, a boutique dedicated to all things plastic.

Margaret remembered the old shopkeepers forced out by the rising rents. Apparently you needed to sell two-thousand-dollar dresses and distinctly odd candles to afford the neighborhood now.

They reached June's, one of those trendy cafés where you ordered dinner at the counter, then waited an eternity for the waiter to deliver it. They stared hungrily into the glass case filled with white platters of roasted vegetables and pastas and meat loaf. After careful consideration, they made their selections and searched for a table.

Seated on the sidewalk under blazing heat lamps, they watched the traffic creep west towards Beverly Hills. "These new stores are like SUVs," remarked Margaret. "They muscled their way onto the block and no one can stop them."

"You'll outlive them," said Lilly. "You've been here twenty years which, in LA time, means you're an institution."

Two stylish young women in jeans and knee-length coats sat at the adjacent table, chatting away on separate cell phones. Their beet salads arrived, placed before them by a scruffy young man with a smear of food on his chin. Upon closer inspection, Margaret realized it wasn't leftovers—it was a bulbous silver stud.

Breathing in the carbon monoxide from hundreds of idling engines and listening to the cacophony of barking cell phone conversations, Margaret wasn't sure that maintaining an institution in Los Angeles was a worthy pursuit. Did anyone really notice a cup of tea awash in an ocean of lattes?

She drove back to her house on Sierra Bonita, past the clusters of young actors outside the kickboxing gym and the Coffee Bean.

Three drivers cut her off. Then the van behind her honked furiously when she declined to join the herd stealing the left hand turn through the red light at Fairfax.

When the signal changed to green, Van Guy swerved around her, cutting across oncoming traffic. "Fucking bitch!" he screamed.

Dazed and shaking, Margaret made it home and sat, for a while, on her porch in the backyard. She tucked a wool blanket around her legs and listened to the crickets and the drone of her next-door neighbor's television set. Finding the balance in LA—what you could live with, what you couldn't—was a daily, if not hourly, struggle. She wondered if other citizens in the world wrestled with their cities as much as people here.

Probably just the older people, she thought.

She remembered living in London when Tony was starring in *Hair* and she was working in the box office. They were madly in love but always breaking up because he wouldn't get married and spent all his money on cocktails and clothes.

Malcolm, the intensely artistic director, fancied her. She tried desperately to fall in love with him but his small penis and rather dull lovemaking kept her from accepting his repeated marriage proposals. Clearly he saved his genuine passion for the theater, as his idea of foreplay was to mumble her name, declare that she was quite beautiful, and then lie down, limply, on top of her.

Now I'd be the wife of a British knight, she thought, with a country house and a private jet. Instead, I'm the ex-wife of a gorgeous gay has-been.

How could she have been so stupid about sex and marriage?

Later that night in Silver Lake, Lilly was in her cheerful kitchen baking three coffee cakes. The Swedish cabinet doors were ajar and the bamboo floor was gritty with sugar and flour. On her way home, she had dropped off Deborah's boots at the shoe repair and picked up Deborah's glasses at the optician down on Hyperion.

No wonder we barely have sex anymore, thought Lilly. I'm her goddamn mother.

Deborah was hosting a meeting in her office in the morning. The fierce competition among the network executives manifested itself in The Breakfast Meeting. It was no longer enough to have a carafe of coffee, some juice, and Danish. Now the spreads featured wicker baskets stuffed with muffins and mini Bundt cakes or theme buffets with Southern cheese grits or New England flapjacks. Last month Deborah's archrival, Priscilla, had set up both a waffle bar and an omelet station.

Lilly mixed up confectioners' sugar with maple syrup, then dripped it lovingly over the golden crusts.

Around ten, Deborah came home from work and admired the cakes. "They're beautiful, Lil, thank you."

She kissed Lilly, kicked off her heels, and then stuck the tip of her index finger in the bowl of frosting for a teensy tiny taste. "They always ask me where I get my coffee cakes but I never tell. I love to see them squirm."

"Yeah, well, after all my effort, they'd better eat them," said Lilly.

"They'll bitch about their carbs and whatever diet they're on . . . then about an hour into it, they'll nosh."

"Should I make something else? Maybe a frittata . . . I could do it in the morning." Lilly always worried there wouldn't be enough. "Remember Priscilla's spread."

"She's number two, so she tries harder," Deborah said. "I'm an executive, not a caterer." She nestled herself against Lilly's round curves. "You take such good care of me," she whispered.

Lilly kissed Deborah's finger, still sticky with the maple glaze, and led her to their bedroom in the back of the house. Just beyond the sliding glass doors, the wind was snapping at the palm fronds, making them both feel restless.

Unbuttoning Deborah's stiff cotton shirt, she reached inside and touched the creamy skin, so warm and supple. She wanted to devour her lover's confidence and energy and keep a little bit of it for herself.

After the love, they sat back against their pillows and reached for their respective bedside reading: a new script for Deborah and the March edition of *Bed and Breakfast* magazine for Lilly.

Snuggling side by side under the goosedown comforter, Lilly interrupted Deborah's concentration to show her the glossy pictures of an innkeeper in Vermont who raised goats and made cheese. "Doesn't she look happy?"

Deborah glanced at the photo of a hearty middle-aged

woman with long gray braids and ruddy cheeks swaddled in three layers of polar fleece.

"She looks freezing." Deborah returned to her script. "Vermont! Winter is nine months long there."

A few pages later, Lilly saw herself riding along with a jolly group of cyclists on a bike tour of California vineyards. "What about Sonoma?" she said. "No snow there."

All was quiet. Deborah was fast asleep.

Gently lifting up the script, Lilly returned it to the stack on Deborah's nightstand. Then she clicked off both their lamps and cozied up against her pillow.

She imagined herself in stiff boots, worn jeans, and a Patagonia barn jacket, tending her herd of silky goats and hosting impromptu wine and cheese parties in the grand living room of a restored Victorian inn.

The scratchy rustle of palm trees gave way to the gentle sound of bleating and the occasional call of the Vermont warbler.

There was nothing like the peace of faraway New England to soothe the frantic spirit of Silver Lake.

Chapter Six

The toilet in the customer bathroom was stopped up. Both Margaret and Lilly had had a go at it but the shit had simply refused to budge. Margaret was tense because:

a. It was a Saturday
b. It was a bridal shower and
c. Blair, the pudgy bejeweled maid of honor, had slipped in the sludge and ruined her pink suede slingbacks.

Some important young head of some important company was marrying some equally powerful someone and thirty fashionable women would all need to pee in the next hour. It was the third shower given for this woman—Chloe? Zoë?—and as Margaret plunged the toilet she mused how remarkable it was that the less you needed wedding gifts, the more you received.

Lilly left ten messages for Sylvia, The Worst Landlady In The World, then suggested to Margaret that they hire their own plumber.

"Then I'll have to pay," said Margaret. "It's Sylvia's responsibility."

"It's your blood pressure," Lilly snorted.

The customers would be forced to use their toilet off the kitchen, which set Lilly on edge.

Blair pushed her way into the kitchen and snapped her fingers at Margaret, who was stacking currant scones on a platter.

"That bathroom smells like crap!" she shrieked. "It's drifting towards my party."

"I can assure you I'm doing all I can," said Margaret, in a soothing tone. "But it is plumbing. This is an old building. Surely you understand."

"I understand that I'm going to be paying substantially less if it's not fixed." Blair added a toss of her big hair to another sharp snap.

Margaret was worried. She didn't want to lose money on a Saturday, her busiest day.

"In the meantime, your ladies may use our restroom here in the kitchen. It's small but clean and serviceable." Margaret opened the bathroom door and Blair stuck her head in, winced, sighed, and grunted.

"Is there anything else I can do?" said Margaret stoically.

A cell phone clanged and Blair waved Margaret aside with a snotty, "Just deal."

An urgent desire to hop into her Volvo and flee swept over Margaret. She was indignant. How dare this woman drive around the twist over what was, really, a minor inconvenience? She'd love to see a community service program where every hateful Amazon with a cell phone was ordered to spend a month in Baghdad using an outdoor privy.

An hour later, Kevin, a willowy man in his late twenties wearing a filthy, black T-shirt and silver studded belt, appeared with his toolbox. He was Sylvia's handyman but really, he was neither.

Lilly's heart sank when she saw him. "Hey Kevin, the toilet up front is broken. But we've got a bridal shower going on, so can you *be discreet*?"

Kevin shrugged in a way that prompted Lilly to clarify. "I mean: don't make a lot of noise."

Lauren, taking an early break in her customary seat on the counter, took a big bite of scone and immediately spat it out.

"Gross! Lilly . . . something's wrong with these."

From her post at the tea-steeping station, Margaret threw an accusing glance at Lilly and made a move towards the offending scone.

"Customer!" Lilly mouthed, jabbing frantically towards the bathroom door.

As if on cue, they heard the toilet flush, the sound of

running water, and then the Bride emerged from the bathroom.

The ladies froze, in tableau, and smiled insincerely at the guest of honor, a thin, coltish woman with enormous brown eyes and equally enormous diamond stud earrings.

"Excuse me!" she whinnied, then skittered past the counters and out the door.

Once she was sure they were alone, Margaret marched over to Lauren and held out her hand for the tainted scone. Passing Lilly an embarrassed look, Lauren relinquished the suspect.

Breaking off a small piece, Margaret nibbled thoughtfully.

"Too much soda."

"It's not my fault!" said Lilly. "There are too many people coming in and out. I can't focus!"

"Lauren, stop eating this instant and retrieve all the scones from the tables," said Margaret. "No one should taste these."

"What am I going to say?"

"Say nothing," said Margaret. "Just quietly remove them."

"Don't worry," said Lilly. "No one pays attention to the help."

Lauren slid off the counter and dragged herself across the room as if carrying a fifty-pound sack of flour.

Opening the freezer, Margaret yanked out a rectangular Tupperware box.

"Lilly, pop these in the oven and I'll mix up another batch right now."

Lilly flipped the lid and peered down at a dozen large scones studded with golden raisins. "There's not enough to feed . . ."

"Cut them in half," ordered Margaret. She was running at full tilt: sifting flour, beating an egg and mixing it up with a little milk. Exasperated, she grabbed the plastic box out of Lilly's hands. "Oh, go help Lauren. I'll finish these."

Lilly scowled but did as she was told. The weirdly sweet scent of pot was wafting down the hall. No way someone's getting high at this shower, she thought. Poking her nose into the bathroom she identified weed, beer, and a tinge of rancid breath. Looking down, she noticed brown, brackish water pooling on the tile floor. Kevin was nowhere in sight.

Racing outside to the parking lot, she spied his van rumbling down the alley. Putting on some speed, she reached him at the street entrance.

"Stop!" She pounded furiously on the driver's door.

Kevin seemed unsure who she was.

"Roll down the window!"

He cracked the glass halfway. A cloud of marijuana smoke escaped.

"You can't leave that toilet!"

"I think the pipe's broke," he said. "I'll come back tonight when no one's there and pull up the tile."

Lilly felt a burst of sweat in her armpits.

"I've got another job," he said, rolling up the window and stepping on the gas.

"And stop getting high on our time!"

Poor Margaret, thought Lilly. She's going to faint.

But Margaret didn't faint. She baked another four dozen scones, took ten pictures of the shower guests with ten digital cameras and, in a supreme act of generosity, sat at the boring relatives' table and chatted with dotty Aunt Anne about the school trip she'd made to England fifty years ago. ("You know what I remember most? The guards at Buckingham Palace never smiled!")

For her part, Lilly patiently endured the silly remarks of thirty women who needed to pee and were rerouted through her domain. ("You must have so much fun, baking cakes all day!" "Is this the way to the little girls' room?" "You know, my kitchen is twice this size but all I ever make is take-out!")

When the party was finally over, Margaret added up the figures, deducted a hundred dollars for shoe cleaning, and presented the charge slip to Blair, who was sitting alone at the bride's table, staring blankly into space.

With a cursory glance at the total, Blair scribbled in a 25 percent tip and, struggling to her feet, gave Margaret a kiss on the cheek. "You're a doll," she said. "I don't know why I got so stressed."

"My dear, a bridal shower is a test of mettle," Margaret said. "And you came through beautifully."

Blair cast down her eyes in the shame of a modern woman who doesn't quite measure up. "But I'm always reading these articles about how you can throw stress-free parties."

"Fiction," said Margaret.

When her employees had said goodbye, and she was standing outside in the cool night air, Margaret became aware of her stiff lower back and burning feet. Arriving home, she dropped her keys and purse on the table in the entryway and made a beeline to the bathroom, desperate for a hot soothing soak.

While reaching for the taps, she remembered it was Kate's birthday tomorrow and she had promised to drive up to Ojai for dinner.

Suddenly, even the effort it would take to fill the tub seemed daunting.

She undressed, crawled into bed, and remained perfectly still for ten hours.

Chapter Seven

Tony and his boyfriend, Michael, had offered to make the birthday dinner but Margaret couldn't remember a time that they had actually delivered on a culinary promise. So on Sunday morning, she picked up a raspberry-filled yellow cake at the pâtisserie; two chickens, rosemary, field greens, red potatoes, and triple cream Brie at the market; then hit the 5 North and its bleak collection of housing developments and fast food restaurants. With relief, she turned onto the 126 to Fillmore, where perfectly aligned citrus groves marched up the hillsides. A few pomegranate trees, with their slender branches and tapered leaves, flanked the highway and farmstands promised everything from Christmas trees to olives and honey.

When she reached the 33 North to Ojai, she realized she could let out her breath.

Up Henderson Road, past the pair of jagged stone pillars, and down a gravel driveway was Tony's place. He had transformed a plain-Jane ranch house into a country showgirl with wooden shutters, gorgeous casement windows, and a river rock path.

The front door was always unlocked, so she pushed inside and dumped her satchel in the guest bedroom on the left, pausing briefly to admire the four-poster cherrywood bed. Tony might have thrown away his career, but he always hung on to the antiques.

She passed through the open living room, with its inviting velvet sofa, leather club chairs, and sooty stone fireplace. A bank of windows revealed an expansive green lawn and oval pool. She could see her daughter and her ex floating on rafts in the tranquil water. Curls of steam flickered around them.

They are bookends, she thought. Kate's wheat-blond hair, creamy complexion, and soft blue eyes were a startling reminder of Tony twenty-five years ago before alcohol and age changed everything.

Opening a glass-paned door, she stepped onto the covered porch and waved.

"Kate! Tony!"

"Darling, come in for a swim," Tony called out in his plummy voice.

"It's February and about sixty degrees." She walked down to greet them.

"But that's summer in England." He paddled his raft around to face Kate. "Is it too early for Pimm's?"

"Daddy!" Kate giggled.

"Just kidding, sweetheart. Perhaps Mummy will make us some tea?"

"Where's Michael?" Margaret asked, shading her eyes from the clear, bright sunshine.

"Yoga. Don't know when he's coming back."

Thank God she'd brought the dinner.

The bright white kitchen with the wide-plank floors was picture perfect and without a scrap of food. There was, however, a large selection of teas and wine.

Tony always preferred a liquid diet.

Margaret put away the groceries and set the kettle on to boil. Kate flitted through the house wrapped tightly in a towel.

"Jesse'll be back soon," she called out. "He went down to the thrift shop. I'm getting dressed."

Margaret set out the tea on a teak table under a weeping pepper tree. Tony poured for both of them.

"Our baby is twenty-eight . . . but we haven't aged," he smiled.

In fleece pullovers and jackets they sat side by side, sipping smoky Earl Grey and watching the sky turn a dusky coral as the sun descended behind the mountains. One of the perks of our divorce, thought Margaret, is that we don't have to chatter.

Having changed into a beige fisherman's sweater and jeans, Kate returned with Jesse, a willowy young man with a perpetual air of dreaminess about him.

Margaret watched them nestle together, their limbs entwined, their matching long blond hair reminiscent of London in the late 60s.

When she had been twenty.

They're so gorgeous, she thought. We must have been, too.

"Did our Kate tell you?" said Tony. "She's leaving for New York."

Margaret's spine fluttered. "New York!"

"Mom, don't freak," her daughter begged.

"Kate, really. It's a bit of a shock."

"Blame it on me," said Jesse, "I can't leave her behind."

The plans were revealed: Jesse had found an old storefront in a fashionable Hudson Valley town where they were going to sell antiques and do design work. It was close to Manhattan, where he had lots of friends and potential clients.

While murmuring support and good cheer, Margaret felt sick and starved. She clasped her hands in her lap for fear that she'd jump up and hold Kate back. But as the couple spoke excitedly about the adventure, she recognized the rapture on Kate's face and she understood. Her daughter was setting off with an exquisite young man; a prince, really.

It had grown cold and dark. Jesse and Kate collected the tea dishes and hurried back inside, casting the parents from their spirited wake.

"Oh, dear," Margaret said softly.

Tony reached for her bottled-up fists and cupped them gently with his thin, graceful hands.

"Darling, don't despair. It was bound to happen. We all run away from home. Even if it's a lovely home." He spread his arms wide, indicating the house, the pool, and the avocado groves beyond.

Margaret frowned at him accusingly. "I can't imagine where she developed a knack for the antique business."

"Maggie, it could have been much worse. She could have inherited my acting gene, you know."

By six o'clock, everyone had drifted to the living room. Jesse was piling up logs in the stone fireplace; Tony and Kate were hunched over the backgammon set; Margaret was curled up on the honey-colored sofa, fantasizing that someone else would tend to dinner and give her the night off.

"Hello! I'm home!" The front door slammed.

Michael made his entrance. Thirty, lean and artfully sloppy, he was wearing yoga pants, suede flip-flops, and a Rasta knit cap. A handsome young friend in virtually the same outfit stood slightly behind him.

"Everyone, this is Ben, my best student! He wanted to see the view from up here."

Margaret, Kate, and Jesse said hello. Tony ignored the newcomer.

"Today is Kate's birthday," said Michael.

"Oh, I should go," said Ben, not very convincingly.

"Yes," agreed Tony.

"No, stay for dinner," said Michael.

Margaret shot Tony a wicked smile. "What exactly are our dinner plans?"

Tony turned accusingly to Michael. "You were going to market after yoga, dear . . . but I guess you became distracted." He glanced sharply at Ben, who flinched and then departed for a self-guided tour of the house.

"You always do this to me!" said Michael. "You said you'd handle it!"

This is worse than I expected, thought Margaret. They're already fighting in front of people.

"I won't let you down, Katie," said Tony. "What would you like for dinner?"

Kate smiled feebly at Tony . . . then turned to her mother who was grinning slyly.

"Mom," she said with relief. "Thank god for Mom."

At the center island, under a canopy of hanging copper pots, Kate quartered potatoes while Margaret whisked the vinaigrette. Jesse offered to roast the chickens.

"Are you sure you can manage?" Margaret was slightly dubious.

"He cooks for me all the time," said Kate.

"My mom was big on breaking the gender rules," said Jesse, expertly coating the birds with olive oil, minced garlic, and a squeeze of lemon. "I went to one of those preschools where the boys were encouraged to play with dolls."

Margaret was duly impressed. But when he offered to set the table it was a little unnerving.

By nine o'clock the hens were picked clean and Tony was slurring. They resumed their circle around the fireplace to watch Kate open her presents. Michael and Tony showered her with expensive leather goods—a datebook, matching wallet, cell phone case, and tote—and Margaret realized the benefits of having two dads.

Then, from the corner of her eye, she caught Michael groping Ben as they snuggled together on the plush sofa.

Jumping up, she scurried to the kitchen, brewed some strong espresso, and when she returned, announced charades.

Ben was embarrassing at improv, stuttering and flapping his arms in despair. Tony was brilliant as he deftly acted out *The Maltese Falcon* and *Meet Me in St. Louis*, the latter leading him into a camp medley of show tunes that left them aching with laughter.

Margaret watched quietly as Michael fell out of lust with Ben and into love with Tony again.

Then she called it a night and retreated to her room with its homey chenille bedspread and pin-striped wallpaper. On the walls were framed lobby cards of Tony in several of his films in the 70s. She made a pilgrimage around the perimeter: there he was as a rakish London mod; here he's a medieval knight; a 1920s dandy; a Dickensian ruffian.

I always adored him in costume, she thought sweetly.

The next morning, after breakfasting on leftover baguette and jam, mother and daughter hiked the Thatcher Trail to the top of the Topa Topa Mountains.

"Mom . . . are you mad at me for leaving?" Kate asked as they looked out over the snug green valley.

"I'm mad at you for not telling me," said Margaret.

"Jesse's tired of LA," she said. "He wants to go back to the East Coast. Already he's got two clients in Manhattan that want him to do their apartments."

"But what's in it for you, darling?"

"I'm going to run the store," said Kate. "I want a place of my own . . . like Magpie's. Only without the tea parties."

"He reminds me a bit of Tony," Margaret said, with a slight hint of concern.

"I know." Kate smiled.

Margaret marveled that Kate never judged her father. How is it that she only sees the brilliant actor, the witty raconteur lording over the manor?

"You're sure Jesse's not gay?" she finally asked.

Kate groaned. "Mom!"

Then, "Definitely not!"

"Let's hope your . . . intuition is more developed than mine was at your age."

"He's like the best part of Dad," said Kate.

"And you always see the best in your father," said Margaret.

"And I see the best in my mother," said Kate, throwing her arms around Margaret's shoulders. "Except your paranoia about my boyfriend being gay."

Margaret was overcome with love for her sunny daughter.

With Kate, there would always be something perfect between her and Tony.

⊱✦⊰

At eleven she was packing up her bag when Tony stumbled into her room, bleary eyed and elegant in a royal blue robe.

"Make me coffee?" He threw her that charming grin.

"Isn't that Michael's job now?"

"He's teaching this morning . . . the advanced yoga students."

"Is Ben in that class?" Margaret said pointedly.

"Oh, him!" Tony flicked his hand dismissively.

" 'Him' was unusually friendly with Michael on the sofa last night."

"And so clever of you to start charades," said Tony. "I adore you for it."

Margaret hesitated, then closed up the satchel. "I've got to go."

On the drive back to the city she thought about how everyone was moving on but her. Kate had Jesse and now, apparently, a business to launch. Tony had Michael . . . for the time being until Michael found another, probably less difficult partner.

What do I have? she wondered. A tearoom.

As she passed Magic Mountain and descended into the smog and gloom of Sylmar, she remembered the rolling hills of Shropshire.

A few minutes later, traffic slowed to a crawl. She stared out at the soul-crushing malls of Burbank and wished it were pastureland with cows and a meandering river.

But England was so far away and a lifetime ago.

Who knew if there were any rivers left?

Chapter Eight

*G*ood morning, I think it is morning there. This is
Rosemary Reedsdale calling . . ."

Clarissa was sitting at the pine desk, dutifully
listening to messages when her cell rang. Squinting at the
answering machine, she pressed several buttons before the
tape stopped, then she flipped up her phone. It was her
friend Annie with a tip: the casting director on *Lavender
and Lace* was Glori Guinness.

She sprinted to the kitchen and accosted Lilly, who was
carefully releasing a round yellow cake from its pan.

"Do you know Glori Guinness? She's gay."

The cake plopped out onto the pastry wheel with a large
crack down the middle. Lilly was pissed. "Do you know
every straight person in this town?"

"All the lesbians know each other."

"Why should I do you this favor?"

Clarissa took a deep breath. "Because this is my last audition."

Lilly rolled her eyes. Clarissa said this every time she actually had an audition. "I don't know her."

"What about Deborah?"

"I don't mix business with my personal life."

"But everyone does!"

That's why everyone has a shitty personal life, thought Lilly, doing her best to gently press the cake back together.

A half hour later, Margaret pulled into the back alley next to Kevin's van. She could see him talking on the phone. Climbing out of her car, she planted herself directly in his sightline and waited for him to finish, but he ignored her.

He's going to have to come in and face that toilet sometime, she thought angrily. Striding over to his window, she rapped on the glass and pointed towards her tearoom. Startled, he looked at her and held up his index finger in that infuriating *I'll just be a moment* salute.

Margaret had no patience for such blatant signs of disrespect. "I want that bathroom finished today," she said sharply.

Once inside Magpie's, she considered ringing up her landlady to discuss Kevin's fondness for getting high at work, but decided it wouldn't compel him to move any faster.

"Good morning, ladies," she said to the girls in the kitchen.

She noticed Lilly beating frosting and Clarissa shredding cooked chicken. Satisfied that the prep was under way, she headed up to the front desk.

Picking up the message pad her eyes grew large. The name Rosemary Reedsdale was scrawled across the top. She flipped the pages of the booklet back and forth. Good god, where was the rest of the message? When was she coming? When did she call? There were no other notations on the paper. Hastily, she pushed the play button on the machine, but the mechanical voice announced "You have no messages." Breathless, she dashed back to the kitchen.

"Who took the messages?"

"Oh, sorry, I forgot about the machine," said Clarissa, adding curry and mayo to the chicken. "My phone rang and I stopped it."

"Did you hit erase?"

"No, I hit stop."

"I expect you hit erase." *You stupid wretched girl.*

Lilly and Clarissa dropped their work. Margaret was taking a tone.

"All you wrote was 'Rosemary Reedsdale.' Do you have any idea who that is?"

Lilly and Clarissa shook their heads like guilty schoolgirls.

"She is the editor of *Tea Talk* magazine. *Tea Talk* magazine." Somehow, Margaret's accent had become even more English.

"So, that's wonderful," said Clarissa.

"Indeed. I have been waiting for a call from *Tea Talk* for

twenty years and you've erased the bloody message." Margaret was wringing her hands.

"Did you star sixty-nine?" said Clarissa, hurrying back to the machine. She pressed every button three times. "You need a new machine! One that doesn't accidentally erase messages."

Margaret stood behind Clarissa, her arms folded across her chest and her teeth clenched.

Clarissa began to babble. "All the buttons are too small. They're impossible to see."

"Were you wearing your glasses?"

"That's just for driving." Collapsing into the desk chair, Clarissa clutched herself and sobbed. "You're right, I'm old. I'm old and I'll never, ever get that audition. And now I don't even have an agent!"

Margaret felt torn between slapping her silly and scooping her up in a motherly hug.

"The world of acting is, indeed, quite daunting. However . . . while you are in the tearoom, our customers, and their messages, must come before everything else."

Clarissa sniffled. "I know. I'm really, really sorry. It's just this audition. It's . . . you don't know how much I need it. I'm sorry I'm so distracted—I never bring my problems to work. I'm a very loyal employee."

In a way, thought Margaret. *Considering everything I have to put up with.* She noticed that Clarissa's mascara was pooling in the lacy wrinkles under her eyes.

"Go on now and fix your makeup," she said gently.

Clarissa shuffled into the customer restroom where she

discovered Kevin, sitting on the floor amongst broken tile reading *Guitar* magazine. Annoyed, she followed Margaret back into the kitchen and locked herself in their tiny bathroom.

"So, what happened?" said Lilly, smearing her cake with creamy white icing.

Margaret peered halfheartedly into the bowl of chicken curry, then added chutney and a sprinkle of raisins. "She deleted Rosemary."

"Well, let's call her back."

"Call her back and say we're so incompetent that we lost her message?" Really! Americans always believed that a whiny "sorry" was sufficient. Had they any standards at all?

But Lilly snatched up the wall phone and asked directory assistance for the London area code. In thirty seconds she had *Tea Talk*'s number.

"Here," she said, handing Margaret the receiver. "Just blame the machine."

"What if it wasn't her?"

"Blame the machine."

With each transatlantic ring, Margaret's heart paused. After six agonizing tones, the *Tea Talk* answering service picked up. Of course! They were hours ahead and no one was in the office.

Feeling self-conscious, Margaret turned her back to Lilly and hunched over the phone. "Hello, this is Margaret Moore at Magpie's Tearoom in Los Angeles. I am calling to confirm a reservation for Ms. Reedsdale. I do hope you'll ring back at your earliest convenience, as our phone machine didn't quite catch the time. I do apologize. You understand modern technology and its limitations. Well . . . looking forward to your visit . . . well, then, goodbye." Her steely command of the language faded into a tiny mouse squeak.

"There, you see? Nothing to it," said Lilly. "I'm sure this happens all the time." She reached out to pat Margaret reassuringly on the arm but her boss recoiled.

"Margaret," Lilly said. "Let's be happy about this. It's a good thing."

Margaret said nothing. She wished she could stifle the trepidation she felt about Rosemary's impending visit.

Perched uncomfortably on the toilet seat, Clarissa used the pretense of fixing her face in order to work her cell phone. She called Mimi, a director who cast her two years ago. ("I was the guest star who played the psychic foster mother?") Then Jason, an actor she worked with three years ago. ("How's your vegan theater company?") She left messages on four other cell phones, then emerged to badger Lilly.

"What if I call Deborah? If I get the part it'll make her look good."

"You are determined to ruin my cake," said Lilly. She was in a very delicate stage, affixing coconut curls atop three perfectly frosted layers. "Deborah doesn't need you to look good—she's gorgeous. They push and shove to get a spot next to her in Power Yoga."

Lauren breezed in with the ubiquitous cigarette. "Sorry I'm late. I had an audition."

"Put that out," said Margaret. "Do I have to engage the bloody fire extinguisher?"

"An audition for what?" asked Clarissa.

"This pilot, *Lavender and Lace,*" said Lauren.

Clarissa gasped, then grabbed a tray of sandwiches and stomped out of the kitchen.

"What's with her?"

Margaret and Lilly exchanged stony glances.

"Lauren, I need you to empty the dishwasher," said Margaret. "Hurry, please."

"No prob," said Lauren, tamping out her cigarette on the kitchen counter and stashing it back in the pack.

All afternoon, Clarissa fumed. Lauren had auditioned for her pilot! She was curt to the mother and daughter next to the fireplace and mixed up all the orders of the school fundraising committee next to the windows. She vowed never to speak to Lauren ever again.

Margaret and Lilly did their best to remain outside Clarissa's orbit and limited the conversation to the work at hand.

Lauren sailed easily around Clarissa's bad vibes. She was used to the petty jealousies of other women and had been told by her mother, Vicky, that it was the price one paid for being totally gorgeous.

It was pouring rain when Clarissa headed home that night, and Laurel Canyon was jammed with commuter traffic. She could feel her stomach snap with every lurch of the car as it inched its way up the muddy, rock-strewn road.

After forty minutes she turned onto Lookout Mountain Drive, which was now a stream of water cascading down the hill. Guiding the Jeep up her narrow, twisting street, she stopped briefly at her mailbox before charging up a steep crumbling driveway.

The House That Buck Love Bought was a sagging shingled cabin with peeling paint and a spectacular view of the canyon. It also had a decade's worth of termite infestation and rotting wood that Clarissa couldn't afford to fix. She knew she should probably sell it and bank the profit but she was attached to her house and her eclectic neighborhood.

Entering the living room, she heard the plop of water smacking the hardwood floor from the ceiling above. If only she could book a few jobs! God, she needed money.

She thought of Mark's house with its brand-new, watertight roof and was miserable. In the kitchen, she flipped on the light and felt pure hatred for the fake brick linoleum floor and the cheesy particle board cabinets from the 70s. She dumped her purse and mail on the scratched Formica counter, then fetched a can of soup from the cupboard next to the stove.

When I moved in, I was going to turn this house into a beautiful little jewel box, she thought, emptying the orange viscous goop into a saucepan. It never occurred to me that I wouldn't have a brilliant career. The explosion of recently remodeled houses in her neighborhood was a daily reminder of her crushing failure. Sometimes driving past the contractors and the painters she wondered what her neighbors thought of her own decaying dwelling. Did they pity her? Did they point her out as a cautionary tale and say, "That's what happens when your show gets canceled after two seasons and doesn't go into syndication"?

Or were they waiting, like vultures, for her house to sink into foreclosure so they could get it for nothing, tear it down, and build a ten-thousand-square-foot Tuscan villa?

While the minestrone warmed, Clarissa shuffled through her mail. She pushed aside the bills and three solicitations from realtors and picked up the *Hollywood Reporter*.

On page three, the headline *Lavender and Lace* jumped out. Why was this show haunting her? Unable to stop herself, she read down to the show credits and spied a familiar name. *Cabbie Schiffman*.

"Oh my god!" She snapped off the gas burner. A tidal wave of hope carried her across the living room and into her frilly bedroom with its rosy sponged walls and ivory lace comforter.

A large sliding aluminum window revealed a dark canyon dotted with oaks and manzanita. Directly underneath the glass was her altar, a narrow bench crowded with precious icons and candles. Taking a deep, cleansing breath, she knelt down before her beloved statues of Buddha, Quan Yin, and the Black Madonna. She caressed a large amethyst crystal and the stones she had collected from Plum Island, back in Massachusetts.

Then she picked up a blue velvet bag that was filled with amulets. "Divine mother," she whispered softly. "Please guide me in my art, my acting life, at this crucial time."

Reaching inside, she sifted through the stones and withdrew the one that felt right. Excitedly, she turned the talisman face up in her right palm. It was Spider Goddess, the sign of creativity ready for expression!!

My luck has changed, she thought. With a sense of hope and gratitude, she gently closed her eyes and repeated her affirmations.

Cabbie Schiffman will see me and I will get a job and I will serve the greatest good.

As a final act of empowerment, she lit the emerald green Prosperity candle and then returned to her soup.

The next morning while driving to work, Clarissa told herself to detach from Lauren. Remember, she's a terrible actress and it doesn't matter what auditions she gets. *Cabbie Schiffman will see me and I will get a job and I will serve the greatest good.*

The three employees were alone, as Margaret was stuck at home waiting for the cable repairman. It was Wednesday, their slow day, and it was still raining. It would have been a good day for Kevin to work on the bathroom, but he had called with another bogus excuse—something about not having the part until tomorrow.

They'd turned on the fire and the tearoom was warm and cozy. With only four customers there wasn't much for them to do. Clarissa had lots of time to think about getting that audition.

"I know one of the producers on *Lavender and Lace*," she confided to Lilly as they were slicing ham for the French

Ham and Marmalade sandwiches on soft white bread. "He was the production assistant on *Detective Buck Love*."

Whipping out her cell, she dialed the production office. "Cabbie Schiffman, please."

Lilly hoped Cabbie's memory was exceptional. Fifteen years in television was at least five generations back.

While on hold Clarissa whispered, "I think he once had a crush on me."

Yeah, when you were twenty-five, Lilly thought. You better hope he likes older, desperate women now.

"Cabbie Schiffman's office." A bright young man came on the line.

"This is Clarissa Richardson," she said boldly. "I'm an old friend of Cabbie's and I'd like to audition for the part of Scarlett Finnegan."

"Just have your agent call," said Todd, the overeducated assistant.

Clarissa's confidence developed a crack. "Well . . . I just left my agent—you know how that is! I'm interviewing with other agencies but I haven't decided on one yet."

"Hmmm," said Todd.

"Cabbie knows my work."

"Hmmmmmm," said Todd again. His brightness faded.

"I starred on *Detective Buck Love*. Cabbie was the production assistant on that show."

There was a long silence. Didn't he remember the show?

"It was a very big show."

"I don't doubt it," said Todd, with a wink in his voice. "Melissa, give me your cell. I'll pass it on to Cabbie."

After carefully reciting her number, Clarissa snapped the phone shut and beamed at Lilly. "I'm in!"

"You got the audition?"

"Not yet . . . I left him my number. But I'm sure he'll call. I mean, I was Wanda."

"Well, Wanda, were you nice to him back then?"

"Of course. I'm a total pro."

"You sound like a stalker," said Lauren, dumping a tray of dishes on the counter.

Forgetting her earlier promise to detach, Clarissa's green eyes narrowed. "Some people think acting requires more than working out at the gym."

"You gotta prepare for the nude scene." Lauren pulled a pack of cigarettes out of her jeans' pocket.

"Margaret forbids that," said Clarissa.

"She's not here."

"Take it outside." Lilly gently pushed Lauren out the back door.

"But it's raining."

"There's an awning." Then, against her better judgment, she resumed her conversation with Clarissa.

"Don't remind Cabbie he was a production assistant. People in this town like to bury their past lives. That's why they never do you any favors once they've reached the top."

"That's not true!" said Clarissa, her jaw dropping. "People in power are always doing favors for each other."

"Only if the other person is powerful, too." Lilly realized, too late, that she had crossed over into Harsh Reality Land, a place Clarissa was loathe to visit.

"You're trying to sabotage my audition!" Clarissa's voice was climbing into the ozone layer.

"I'm trying to help you." Lilly chewed her thumbnail, mulling it over. "If you're running for mayor, it's okay to be the poor kid who's come up from nothing. But in Hollywood, everyone wants instant success. All the time."

Before Clarissa could respond, Lauren opened the back door and hissed, "Oh, I forgot . . . your window table wants more fucking cream."

Happy to end her conversation with Lilly, Clarissa grabbed the jar of Devon cream from the fridge. She scooped a buttery mound into a dainty bowl and quickly left the room.

Back from the smoking section, Lauren checked on a tray of scones in the oven. "Those are way flat."

Lilly bristled. "They're not always puffy."

"Don't worry, I won't tell Margaret. I don't give a shit." Lauren inspected a platter of white sandwiches with melon-colored cream weeping between the slices. "Why are those orange?"

"I whipped up mango with some Devon cream. Try one."

"Way too much fat," said Lauren.

Reason 10,001 to leave this city, thought Lilly. Small talk about fat content passes as actual conversation.

At five, all the customers were gone and the girls decided to clean up early. Loading the dishwasher, Clarissa leaned over to Lilly, "I appreciate your concern but I can't go to a place of fear. We all create our own reality."

That is the truth, Lilly thought.

"Anyway, Cabbie has worked his way up to being a producer and he should be proud. Everyone loves to hear a success story." She jammed more dirty spoons into the packed utensil basket.

People in Los Angeles hate to hear your success story, Lilly thought silently. They'd rather see you fired and take your job.

But she said nothing.

Lilly set the security alarm and they all stepped outside. The rain had scrubbed the sky until it shone sapphire blue. Even the parking lot smelled fresh.

"I've gotta run," said Clarissa, "I want to go over my scene before class."

"You take a lot of classes, don't you?" said Lauren.

"I like to prepare."

"How much preparation does it take to say, 'What are we going to do now, Detective?'"

Clarissa whipped around. How dare this idiot attack her work, her methods? She was ready to lash out, when she remembered her mantra: Don't let her get to you. She's beautiful but she has no talent. No training at all.

Clarissa drew herself up into twenty years of experience and climbed into the Jeep. As she switched on the radio and settled into her seat she thought, I am a great actor and I know my craft. Even if the world doesn't acknowledge me, I know it is true.

It was what she would cling to all the way to her class.

As soon as Clarissa's car disappeared down the alley, Lilly turned to Lauren. "Would it kill you to be a little nicer," she said, locking the back door.

"So now you're taking her side?"

"I'm not on anyone's side. I just think we should all support each other."

"Why?" Lauren snapped. She hopped into her dinged-up Explorer and sped away.

Lilly stuck her hands on her hips. Oh my god, she realized, there it is! The final reason I should leave this town: All I meet are bitches.

Chapter Nine

The room reeked of herbal body lotion and nervous sweat. A dozen blond-babe-twentysomethings were seated on sharp metal folding chairs studying their lines.

Lauren sized up the competition and felt anxious. She wasn't sure if she was the most beautiful one there.

They were battling for a small role in an action movie. Her character Annika plays strip poker with a cop named Blade and his adorable Jack Russell terrier.

I've never played strip poker in real life, Lauren thought.

But, whatever.

She glanced at her lines, then dug in her purse for a compact mirror to check her makeup. A girl she knew from spinning class entered the room and sat down next to her.

"Hi, Lauren," Lisa said nervously. "The town seems really quiet. Are you working?"

Lauren easily dismissed this question. Who would ever truthfully answer it?

"I've got a callback on a pilot tomorrow."

A shadow of pure hatred flicked briefly across Lisa's face. Then it was gone and the insincere support kicked in.

"That's so great."

That'll shut her up, Lauren thought.

Vicky had schooled her in ruthlessness. Her mother saw every other woman as a competitor in her own private beauty pageant.

"You should go to LA," Vicky had told her. "You're just as pretty as the girls on TV."

Lauren didn't need the push. After seventeen years of Vicky's jobs (twelve) and Vicky's husbands (four), she'd been ready for flight.

"But you've got to change your last name," Vicky said, shuddering. "I mean Blodgett is god awful, and it reminds me of your father. Why don't you use your middle name? It sounds like somebody famous."

"Lauren Savannah." Dana, the casting director, stood at the door holding a clipboard.

Entering the inner sanctuary, Lauren faced five men sitting behind a folding banquet table: the producer, the writer, the director, and two guys of indeterminate title. The producer's assistant stood next to a video camera waiting to capture her performance.

"Can you tell me anything about my character?" Lauren asked hopefully. She had heard other actors use this line and she thought it sounded professional.

"The terrier and Annika are looking at their cards. The terrier barks that he's good. Blade looks at Annika. Now take it from there," squeaked the wiry, nerdy director.

Thanks for the fucking clue, Lauren thought. She felt a rising panic and, with a surgeon's precision, cut it off.

Dana picked up her script. "I'll read the part of Blade the cop. Ready?" The red light of the camera flicked on.

"'You want me to hit you again?' " said Dana.

"'Hit me twice," Lauren said. "'I can take it.'"

"'I hope you know what you're doing . . .' "

Lauren became distracted by the hum of whispering. She glanced at The Table and caught the writer and the director in quiet conversation. Fuck! I must be awful, she thought.

"Can I start again?" she said.

The director exhaled loudly. "No! Just pick it up from here."

Lauren looked back at the script, opening her eyes wide. "'Oooh, you weren't supposed to give me those cards!'" she squealed.

She searched the men for their reaction. The producer was checking his BlackBerry and one of the two nameless guys had left the room. Focus! she told herself. With determination standing in for talent, she forged ahead.

"'The terrier's got two aces . . . so you know what that means,'" Dana said.

"'It means,'" said Lauren, "'I'm going to have to take off my top.'"

Peeling off her T-shirt, she felt the power of her breasts capture the room.

Who needs that stupid script, she thought triumphantly. Now I have everyone's attention.

The crate of watercress, parsley, and lemons she delivered to Magpie's was light compared to most of her other stops.

"Fred's Finest," Stephanie called out. When no one answered she placed the box next to the fridge and stole a peek around the kitchen. There was a polished silver tea caddy and dainty china cups on the sideboard. What's this? she wondered, picking up a tiny quilt with ribbons.

"That's a tea cozy," said Margaret, bustling into the room. "You tie it around the pot to keep the tea nice and warm."

Dropping the cozy, Stephanie blushed. "Sorry, I just . . . have never been in a tearoom."

"My dear, come with me."

As they toured the front room, Margaret explained the ritual.

With the High Tea you started with sandwiches: cucumber, ham, salmon, and egg. This was followed by freshly baked scones, imported Devon cream, and jam. Then a sweet to finish: coconut cake, lemon tart, petits fours, or perhaps shortbread, depending on the mood of the chef. Every lady had her own pot of tea, either black (served with milk and sugar) or herbal (served with lemon and honey).

"If they order the Royal Tea, we add a glass of Champagne or sherry," Margaret said.

This is nothing like produce, Stephanie thought. With her parents and brothers, she worked in a cement warehouse with stark walls and damp floors. She knew the kitchens of many fancy restaurants but never saw the dining rooms.

"Always put a bit of milk in the cup before you pour in the tea," said Margaret. "It's a tradition left over from the days when the hot liquid could crack delicate china."

Stephanie was drawn to the quiet formality. She longed to nestle into the chintz armchair next to the warm fire; to breathe in the aroma of sugary cakes and scones and sip fragrant tea with a friend.

"This place is so beautiful," she said.

Back in the kitchen, Margaret wrapped up a slice of cake and a scone and pressed them into Stephanie's hand. "For your afternoon tea."

My tea, thought Stephanie. The idea was unique. She studied Margaret's kind eyes and smart gray sweater set. "Thank you," she said simply, then, picking up her empty crate, she sailed out the back door.

Stephanie has a natural elegance, Margaret thought.

Especially compared to this one.

Lauren scuffed into the room in sharp-toed boots. Her low-cut corduroys revealed the Three Graces tattoo featured above her round juicy buttocks. She mouthed a silent hello at Margaret and then shrieked into her cell phone.

"Strip-poker with a dog! Isn't that hilarious?"

I am too old for this, Margaret thought, on her way to check the messages. With a sigh, she touched the answering machine.

"This is *Tea Talk* magazine calling. Will you reserve a table for Rosemary Reedsdale on Friday at four o'clock? Thanks so much! Ciao!"

Margaret was dazed. She played the message twice, just to be sure.

It was true! Rosemary was indeed coming. Suddenly the ennui and despair she had felt over Lauren, and perhaps life in general, vanished. She was filled with a robust sense that Things Were Finally Going Her Way. I must check the sherry, she thought. I don't think we have anything worthy of *Tea Talk* magazine. Putting pen to paper, she quickly had a list of urgent requirements that included fresh flowers and a thorough scrub of the bathroom.

Oh my god, she thought. The bathroom.

Hurrying back to the kitchen, she collected her three employees.

"Girls, I have an announcement. Rosemary Reedsdale is coming tomorrow!"

Lilly dropped her jaw. "Wow! Now aren't you glad we called them back?"

"That's wonderful," said Clarissa.

"Who's Rosemary?" said Lauren.

Margaret pressed her hands together. "We have one day, one day! to prepare." She looked at Lilly. "Have we heard from Kevin? Rosemary cannot see that broken loo."

"I'll call his cell," said Lilly, reaching for the phone. But before she could dial they heard the back door slam and the rattle of a metal toolbox. Kevin, still sporting the same black T-shirt of three days ago, glanced into the kitchen.

· "Hey," he said absently, then headed down the hall.

"He looks stoned," said Clarissa. "Shouldn't we call the landlady?"

"No," said Margaret. "I expect an altered state might improve his performance." Then she lowered her voice. "He cannot leave until the toilet is in proper working order."

"Let's box in his van and make him our prisoner," Lilly said gleefully.

Margaret waved her hand dissuasively. "That will not be necessary. He will not be left alone."

All morning they took shifts, hovering by the bathroom door, checking Kevin's work. Slowly and clumsily, he covered over the hole in the floor with smears of wet cement. At lunchtime he mumbled about going out for a chili dog, but Lilly handed him a plate of sandwiches and instructed him to finish.

Meanwhile, Lauren was dispatched to the wine store on Melrose to buy a good bottle of sherry (up to fifty dollars), while Clarissa hand-washed the crystal glasses they used for special occasions.

By four o'clock the cement was dry and they assembled around the toilet for a test drive. Margaret pushed down on the handle and they watched, tensely, as the tissue paper swirled around the bowl, disappeared from view, and did not reemerge.

The women screamed in delight. For the first time that day, Margaret smiled.

Kevin, who was teetering on the edge of a psychotic episode, was released from service and happily reunited with his van and his pot.

Satisfied that the tearoom was in splendid order, Margaret led her troops out into the alley and embraced the cold evening air. "I expect everyone on time tomorrow," she said, looking pointedly at Lauren.

Weary from the physical and emotional demands of the day, Lauren, Lilly, and Clarissa crawled into their cars and headed towards the safety of their respective homes.

Sitting in traffic on Sunset, Margaret listened to an overwrought account of global warming on National Public Radio. Turning down the volume she thought, I'll buy those yellow roses at the florist's tomorrow. February demands yellow. And I must make the scones. Lilly cannot be trusted with such an important task.

A skinny brunette in a silver battering ram cut her off at Fairfax but tonight, the depressing stories on the news and the rudeness of the drivers around her couldn't spoil her cheerful mood.

Everything is falling into place nicely, she thought, pulling into her driveway.

She should have known better.

Chapter Ten

❧

A splitting headache and its sidekick, nausea, woke Margaret on Friday morning. Only perfectionism coupled with a soupçon of control freak could create such searing misery.

At least it's a warm sunny day, she noticed with some relief. Tailor-made for Rosemary Reedsdale. Brits are always happy to escape the dreariness of London in February.

She picked up a double espresso at the drive-through Starbucks and then washed down two Advil. Feeling fortified, she pressed on to Flowers By David where, unfortunately, the roses were quite insignificant.

"Valentine's Day wiped us out," David explained.

Good god, Valentine's Day? When was that?

For a moment she considered driving around the city in a quest for perfect yellow roses.

The Advil kicked in and reason returned. Stop your whinging, she thought. There are loads of other flowers here.

David presented some ranunculus (a rather meek little blossom, she thought) and some star lilies (too large for the tables).

"How about tulips?" he said, as if suddenly struck by lightning. "They combine elements of stature and grace with a note of simplicity."

"Indeed," she said. "Tulips are brilliant."

Stephanie arrived early with the produce but Lilly immediately spied calamity in the crate.

"Stephanie, these aren't English cucumbers."

Stephanie picked up the waxy vegetable. "The English make special cucumbers?"

"English cucumbers are longer and less seedy. Better for sandwiches."

Stephanie grimaced. "I'll go right back downtown and exchange them." She grabbed the crate then stopped. "Wait—I can't! I've still got four more stops."

Get a grip, thought Lilly. You're making this woman sweat over a stupid vegetable.

"Forget it. We'll be fine without English cucumbers."

"You sure?"

"Yeah, I mean, didn't we fight a war against the English?"

"We did?"

"You know, forget everything I said. We're just having a tough day. Lots of tension."

Stephanie was surprised. "But it's so nice here. So peaceful."

You think this is peaceful? thought Lilly. I compromise my sanity every day.

"Don't believe everything you don't see," was all she said.

An hour later when Margaret arrived, Lilly had baked two dozen scones.

They were brownish.

"What are those?" Margaret trembled.

"Toffee chip scones," said Lilly proudly. "I thought I'd make something special for Rosemary."

Why on earth would she experiment on such an important day, thought Margaret. Really, has she no sense at all?

"We are not serving vile candy scones. It's . . . faddish."

"They serve them at the coffeehouses."

"Long after the coffee crowd has moved on to another gimmick, we'll still be serving my grandmother's scones."

Margaret briefly closed her eyes, which made Lilly nervous.

"Of course. Don't worry . . . I'll make grandma's scones." She hurried to the closet for fresh supplies, then gasped.

"Fuck! I forgot we're out of flour. I thought about it yesterday but then I got sidetracked with Kevin."

Margaret checked her watch.

"Rosemary won't be here till four," said Lilly. "Plenty of time to bake new scones."

"I'll go round to the market, then," said Margaret.

"Hey, while you're there," said Lilly slowly, "you might want to pick up some cucumbers, too."

Even with every bone in her body screaming *this is a bad idea*, Clarissa was determined to visit Cabbie's office before work.

The address was listed in the production pages of the *Hollywood Reporter*. Thankfully, he wasn't on a studio lot where she'd have to deal with a guard and a gate.

Two blocks from Ventura Boulevard, a cluster of white stucco bungalows housed the temporary production offices of temporary companies making temporary pilots. Cabbie's was the last one on the left.

She entered the building and spoke confidently to the pretty young receptionist wearing a headset.

"Hi! I'm Clarissa Richardson, an old friend of Cabbie's."

The receptionist squinted. It was often difficult to size up clients in Hollywood. Some of the most successful actors and writers looked unkempt and some of the losers looked like slick newscasters.

"I'm dropping off my headshot for *Lavender and Lace*."

"You can leave it with me," Reception said, pointing to an inbox overflowing with glossy photos and résumés.

"Cabbie and I worked together on *Detective Buck Love*. It was a very big show. He told me to come by and say hi."

Clarissa waited, her heart pounding. Would she or wouldn't she get in?

She looks sorta familiar, Reception thought, and sort of

frantic like the actresses on Lifetime television. "Let me tell him you're here. Please have a seat."

Clarissa sank down on a scratchy mauve sofa and prayed silently to herself.

I send you love and light, Cabbie Schiffman. May we connect in a powerful way.

"He's not in yet."

Margaret returned with the flour and discovered Lilly alone in the kitchen.

"Where are the girls?"

Lilly looked pained. "They're both going to be late. There's messages on the machine."

Margaret said nothing.

"Don't worry. I've got the sandwiches prepped and, well, at least we have two dozen scones."

"Toffee chip!"

Margaret gripped the counter for support. I can't cope, I simply can't cope, she thought.

But the tearoom was open, women were arriving, and someone had to greet them. Magpie's was booked solid, so Margaret stuck a *Reserved* sign on the table next to the fireplace.

For Rosemary.

The character of Scarlett Finnegan was described as the multimillionaire owner of an NFL team who slept with the players, brewed her own beer, and enjoyed a tempestuous marriage with her third husband.

Lauren was in Macy's hunting down her audition outfit. She was vacillating between a clingy jersey cocktail dress and clingy leather pants when her cell rang.

"Hey, girl," said Jeff, her agent. "The callback's at five-thirty. Plus new sides and they wanna hear you sing."

"What?"

"It's now a quirky drama slash fantasy pilot. With singing."

Singing! Lauren felt woozy. It's not like everyone can sing! Why would he send her out for this? I have no idea what I'm doing, she thought.

"You did the whole musical theater thing?"

"Uh, sure, don't worry."

Frantically, she bought both outfits. If she kept the tags on she could return everything next week.

At eleven o'clock, Cabbie Schiffman arrived. The once slender, curly-haired young man had morphed into a doughy guy wearing a baseball cap and tight leather jacket that pulled across his spreading rump.

Clarissa would never have recognized him but Reception whispered that "some actress" was waiting.

Rising gracefully from her chair, Clarissa smiled.

"Cabbie!" she said in her throaty audition voice. "It's so good to see you."

He did a quick search through his mental casting file.

"I'm sorry . . . how do we know each other?"

"It's Clarissa . . . from *Detective Buck Love*. You know . . . Wanda?"

He looked surprised. "Oh . . ." he began.

"I've been trying to get in to see you . . . to audition for *Lavender and Lace*." Clarissa began to relax when she saw that Cabbie was listening. "I mean, you know me, you know my work . . ."

Then three men in jeans and slouchy jackets entered the room.

"Hey, Schiffman." The shortest one cocked a finger at Cabbie. "You ready?"

"Gotta go. Great to see you," Cabbie said, and quickly followed the writer/director/producer trio behind the double doors.

The world, as Clarissa knew it, ended right there, in Studio City on a sunny Friday morning.

Taking her cue from Cabbie, Reception stood up. "Thanks for stopping by."

Stumbling down the walkway, Clarissa released the agony. She cried all the way back to her car where she discovered a forty-two-dollar ticket for parking on a restricted block.

She sat in the front seat and wept.

I can't go to work. I must get out of here.

Her cell rang and she glanced at the number. Magpie's. Suddenly she remembered something about a . . . critic. "Hello?"

"Where the fuck are you?" said Lilly.

Fresh, painful tears streamed down her face.

"God, are you all right?"

"No . . . my life is over!"

There was something about her tone that Lilly recognized. *Oh, this is an acting thing.*

"You were right about Cabbie Schiffman. I went by his office . . . and he wouldn't see me!"

"Motherfucker."

Clarissa cried harder.

"Look, on any other day I'd say don't come in but . . . Margaret needs you. She's about to split a gut."

"Lilly . . . I can't."

"Clarissa, you must." Lilly paused, searching for the right tact. "Even under the weight of your own tragedy, I know you can give a great performance."

Margaret was easing a tray of hot scones from the oven when Lauren showed up.

"Sorry I'm late but—"

Margaret whipped her head around with a force that cut off Lauren's excuses.

"I'll . . . check the tearoom," Lauren said quickly.

Lilly, filling a mesh tea ball with jasmine leaves, gave Margaret a silent thumbs-up. *Kick some ass, girl.*

When Clarissa arrived a half hour later, her eyes were swollen with sorrow.

She looks like a woman who's learned she has cancer, thought Margaret, checking the temperature on the stainless hot-water urn.

"I'm sorry I'm late," Clarissa said, pausing dramatically. "It will never happen again. I have just come from my very last audition."

Despite her best efforts not to get involved, Margaret felt the gravitational pull of motherhood. "Clarissa, be reasonable. This is not the last audition in the world."

"It was the last one for me."

"I'm confident it's not that bleak."

"I spent my entire life working on my career. And the truth is . . . I don't have one."

"The acting life is formidable . . ." Margaret sighed. "Even when Tony was flying high, the Academy Award nomination, the parties, the interviews, he was riding the depths of depression."

"That was before Paxil," said Clarissa.

"He had stage fright for years after that dreadful competition. The pressure he put on himself to be brilliant was enormous. He could barely speak to the other actors and was drinking the minute he got home."

"I don't have a drinking problem!"

Margaret looked worried. "My dear, are you quite sure you can manage this afternoon?"

Clarissa straightened her back. "I wouldn't let you down on such an important day," she said, dropping her green leather purse on the sideboard. Then she noticed some white pages protruding from Lauren's macramé tote.

Stealthily, she raised them up just enough to read the first two lines.

It was *Lavender and Lace*.

Swinging back into the kitchen with a tray of dirty dishes, Lauren caught Clarissa.

"You took my sides!"

"They were on the sideboard," Clarissa lied brilliantly. "Anyway, that part's not right for you."

"You mean it's too young for you." Lauren wrested the papers from Clarissa's grip and jammed them back in her bag.

Let it go! Clarissa told herself. But the temptation to wound carried her into the minefield. "Scarlett Finnegan sings," she said tauntingly to Lauren. "Do you?"

"Oh just . . . fuck you! You were on a show for about ten minutes twenty years ago. End of story."

Everyone stood still. The ugly truth filled the room and threatened to choke them all to death.

"Last year I played . . . Lady Macbeth!" Clarissa finished lamely.

"Yeah, so what? That doesn't pay the rent."

"It's not about the money. It's about the work. Something you know nothing about."

"I know that I won't be working in a tearoom when I'm forty-five, talking about some sitcom everyone's forgot."

"I'm not forty-five!"

Clarissa burst into tears and locked herself in the bathroom.

Margaret, who had found herself quite immobilized by this scene, suddenly gathered her wits about her. Glaring indignantly at Lauren, she pointed towards the tearoom.

"Go on . . . see to our customers."

With a defiant flip of her hair, Lauren escaped.

"Unbelievable!" Lilly flew to the sideboard and seized the contraband. "This show is ruining our tearoom!"

Unable to stop herself, she read the pages and then looked glumly at Margaret.

"Wouldn't you know . . . this part was made for Clarissa . . . perfect for a thirty-nine-year-old woman. So of course, they'll cast someone ten years younger."

She tucked the sheets back into Lauren's tote and then returned to her jasmine tea.

Margaret stood outside the bathroom door for a moment, then knocked firmly.

"Clarissa, please don't compete with her. You and Lauren are in very different places in your lives. You're on two completely different paths."

Clarissa wailed inside her shelter. "She's on a path. I'm on a cliff."

Margaret appealed to Lilly. "What am I going to do?"

"Push her off," Lilly said firmly. "She's got to face reality some time."

"I do feel for her."

"I used to feel for her. But how long can you hear about someone else's acting career? Let's enact a statute of limitations. It's okay to pursue your dream, but it's against the law to discuss it past the age of forty."

With the toffee chip scones, the run to the market, and the unstable help, Margaret felt her command of life unraveling.

Then at three o'clock, a highly perfumed real estate agent pulled her aside.

"The toilet is stopped up."

God, I hope there's nothing offensive in it, thought Margaret.

She stared into the porcelain bowl. Someone had tried to flush a maxi-pad and it was wiggling around in a revolting sea of bloody water.

Lilly and Margaret plunged the toilet for ten minutes but only succeeded in spilling the foul water all over the floor and themselves.

"Unbelievable!" said Lilly. "What woman in the western hemisphere doesn't know not to flush pads down the toilet?"

"We must get Kevin on the phone now."

"I mean . . . every stall you sit in, there's some Xeroxed sign that tells you not to flush tampons and pads down the toilet."

"Just . . . ring him."

"Fuck, we have that sign!"

"Please!"

Sullenly, Lilly dialed his number.

Kevin's voicemail picked up. She left a message but held little hope that he'd call back.

Taping an "Out of Order" notice on the bathroom door, Margaret felt her spirit break along with the toilet.

At four o'clock the room was packed but no one had identified herself as Rosemary. Two interior-design types declared they'd never come again because she wouldn't give them the *reserved* table.

That was probably a mistake, Margaret thought. Rosemary's not coming. Then she scooped up some dirty dishes and forced that idea from her mind.

At five o'clock, the tearoom was empty.

Margaret stood helplessly in the kitchen doorway, watching her girls quietly clean up. No one had the stomach for conversation.

Lilly shoved the plastic bin of flour under the counter, then crossed the room and gave Margaret an encouraging pat on the arm. "She probably got lost. I'm sure she'll call and reschedule."

Clarissa had resigned herself to the dishwasher, carefully loading the filthy cutlery. Her eyes were dull and her shoulders sagged under the weight of diminished hopes.

Lauren, who had spent the last twenty minutes rearranging cups on the shelf, sidled up to Margaret.

"Is it okay if I leave soon?" she whispered. Then, feigning the utmost concern for her rival's feelings she mouthed, "I have *that* audition."

If I hear the word audition again, I fear I may go mad, Margaret thought, retreating to the tearoom. The front door banged open and a plump woman in her thirties rolled into the room. She had a pierced lip and a splash of crimson acne across her fleshy chest and cheeks.

" 'Ello Luv, I'm Rosemary Reedsdale."

Her lack of refinement was surprising, but Margaret recovered quickly. "Oh, hello! What a pleasure to finally meet you."

"Wha'a brill day I've 'ad, seeing the sights. There a law against ugly people in this town?"

Margaret smiled happily. "It means so much to me to be acknowledged by *Tea Talk* magazine."

Rosemary waved this away and plopped into a chair nearest the door. Margaret resisted the urge to move her to the reserved table.

"Ge'a lot of movie stars in 'ere?"

"A few."

"Any today?"

"No." Margaret began to feel uneasy.

Rosemary frowned. "Pity."

Then she launched into a lively travelogue of all the sights she'd seen that day: Venice Beach, Malibu, the Sunset Strip. She'd bought a Map to the Stars' Homes and had spotted limos and Hummers and dozens of hydraulic, propped-up breasts.

"You must be exhausted," said Margaret. "What you need now is a strong cup of tea."

"Too stuffed for that, Luv," belched Rosemary. "Before I come here, I popped round at that Teaser's down the street. Took a fancy to this coconut mojito."

Margaret spoke weakly. "So, no tea, then?"

Rosemary pulled out her phone and checked for messages.

"But what about my review?"

Rosemary smiled slyly, revealing crooked, dingy teeth. "Don't worry about it."

"Don't worry about it?" Margaret's devotion to good manners began to vanish. "I spent the entire day sick with worry. I held your table for hours. I plunged the loo. I shopped, I made dozens of scones . . ."

"Don't get your knickers in a twist, pet. I don't need tea to write your friggin' review."

Am I the victim of a practical joke? thought Margaret. Some ghastly reality show?

"I'm afraid I don't follow."

"We'll work something out and you'lls get a lovely review."

Noticing Margaret's puzzled face, Rosemary spoke slowly as if addressing a dimwit.

"People sometimes compensate me for my time and all."

The implication was clear, and for a moment, Margaret did consider it. Why not? she told herself. Why not just pay the bitch and be done with this day? What difference would it make?

The difference, she admitted, is that I am Margaret Throssel Moore.

"No," she said simply to Rosemary. "No."

Rosemary gave an embarrassed laugh. "Oh, I see, you think you're better than me . . . acting all high and mighty."

"I think you should leave." Margaret's voice was rising.

"Suit yourself, dearie. But let me tell you, you're livin' in the past."

"Bollocks!"

She yanked Rosemary out of her seat and pushed her to the front door.

"Have you gone mental?"

"Get out of my tearoom!"

Rosemary shook her off. "Well, you can forget about *Tea Talk* magazine! And to think I came all the way over from Malibu!"

Margaret slammed the door and locked it. Leaning her cheek against the wood grain she thought, what have I done? Is she right? Am I completely out of touch?

Sick with doubt, she wheeled around to discover her employees, huddled in the hallway, mouths agape.

"How long have you been here? Spying on me?"

"We were worried," said Lilly.

"We heard voices," said Clarissa.

"You bitches. Well, don't just stand there!"

"What did we do?" Clarissa said, trembling.

"Nothing! You do absolutely nothing! I do it all myself."

Suddenly it was as if she was looking down on them from atop a high perch, desperate to swoop in and tear their flesh with her sharp, vicious claws.

"Get your things and get out," she commanded.

"You're all sacked . . . the tearoom is closed!"

PART TWO

Elsewhere

Chapter Eleven

There are places I remember
All my life
Though some have changed

Lauren sang along with her iPod as she drove to her audition. She had picked a Beatles song because she knew the words and figured everyone loved them. She had spent half the night rehearsing and had persuaded Dakota to film her performance, which quickly evolved from an audition exercise into a sex video.

The melody reminded her of cutting class, hanging out at the lake, smoking, and working at Wet Seal. She didn't especially miss Lakeland but she didn't love LA all that much, either.

When I'm rich I'll love it, she thought. When I have a ton of clothes and a huge house and a trainer. When I'm a famous actress it'll be sweet.

Oops. Here was the off-ramp to Studio City.

Nervousness made her feverish and chilled at the same time. Tilting down the rearview mirror, she checked her armpits and was horrified to discover crescent-shaped sweat stains.

Fuck! Now I can't raise my arms or return the dress. Clumping down the walkway to the bungalow she took two deep breaths and wondered what "being in the moment" meant. Other actors talked about that all the time. Maybe it meant not thinking about the audition too much, which was just fine with her. Thinking about it made her freak.

Inside the reception area, the casting director's assistant, Madison, handed her the new scene:

Scarlett stands on a beach in Malibu, rain beating at her backside. In horror she watches the remnants of her palatial mansion slide down the hill into the Pacific Ocean. Her husband, Rob Harrington, crawls out of the wreckage and wearily climbs into his Range Rover.

ROB

You're like Malibu, Scarlett. You were the place to be. You loved harder and spent more money than all my ex-wives put together. But I can't live in Malibu anymore. It's too . . . expensive.

SCARLETT

You won't beat me, Rob Harrington. It will take more than a mudslide and financial ruin and sex deprivation to bring me down! I am Scarlett Finnegan and I will love again.

Lauren read down a few mores lines, then looked up. "When do I sing?"

"Oh, didn't your agent tell you? We're going another way," said Madison. "Can you do a southern accent?"

"I have to drop class," Clarissa said to Vince DeFaria. She had arrived early at The Company Theater in Los Feliz to speak with her acting coach.

"I lost my day job and I can't afford it right now."

Vince frowned. Clarissa was his best student, a talented actress.

"I was just going for coffee," he said. "Let's talk about it."

They walked down the street to La Muse, a sidewalk café that remained forever faithful to 1950s Paris in its own time warp: coq au vin was on the menu, brooding young writers still read *The Stranger*, and a guy in a navy peacoat was always sketching.

Squeezed between two sets of smokers, Clarissa poured out her story. Vince smiled wryly.

"You think it's funny?" Clarissa was deeply hurt.

"No, no. It's fate. I've been thinking that it was time for you to leave class."

"Leave class?" Clarissa looked bruised.

"The truth is, there's really nothing left for me to teach you."

"But . . ."

"Hear me out." He reached over and cupped her hands. "I want to recommend you for a teaching position."

Teaching? Just when it seemed life couldn't get worse, it did.

"You'd be a fantastic coach, Clarissa. You're a gifted performer and your instincts are amazing."

Flattery piqued her interest.

"UCLA is looking for someone to lead an advanced class. I know the dean over there. He wants an actor with extensive theater credits and I thought of you."

Clarissa was quiet. Now she really missed the tearoom. It was an easy gig that demanded very little.

"Oh, I see," he pulled back. "You think teaching is a comedown."

"No, it's . . . yeah, you're right."

She gave an embarrassed laugh and Vincent's warm brown eyes crinkled. Why doesn't he work more? she wondered. He was handsome and so mesmerizing on stage.

"Don't let pride . . . what you think is beneath you . . . drive your decisions, Clarissa. I know that for you, it's all about the work."

Listen to him, a voice inside her nagged. Vince DeFaria thinks you're great. And if you don't take this job . . . what are you going to do? Wait tables every night? Work a temp job?

"Just consider it. I think their spring quarter begins in a couple of weeks."

He paid the bill and they walked back to the theater.

Suddenly, she felt awash with regret, remembering fifteen years ago when she'd turned down Heavenly Management. At that time, she was pulling in a fortune from *Buck Love*, Ken was her agent, and she couldn't see the point in losing another 15 percent on a personal manager. But it had been a mistake . . . Heavenly's star had risen and then, a year after *Buck Love*, when she was desperate for work, they didn't want her.

Something about this moment felt familiar.

Someone's giving you a chance, she thought. *Yeah, a chance at teaching.*

So what—don't blow it.

"Okay, I'll do it."

Leaning down, he kissed her softly on the cheek, lingering for a moment. It was out of character for him. She had never seen him touch a student before . . . *in that way*.

"Thanks," she said. "I appreciate your help."

"I'm gonna call you, see how you're doing."

She strolled up Vermont Avenue to her car and felt the heat of his gaze following her.

She knew what he was thinking. Now that she was out of class, he could finally sleep with her.

I fear I'm having a nervous breakdown, thought Margaret. But I'm having it the English way, which is to say that I'm alone in my house not speaking to anyone.

For three days she had remained in bed, except for the necessary trips down to the kitchen to warm up canned soup or scramble an egg.

By day four the milk had spoiled and it was time to leave the house, if only to replenish the pantry.

She showered and put on some makeup. Even in her grief and despair, she knew that a woman her age could not pull off the disheveled look so fashionable among the actresses and arty types in her neighborhood. No, a woman past forty needed lipstick, a good haircut, and great-fitting pants when out in public. Otherwise they were simply kidding themselves.

With take-out sushi and a bag of groceries, she drove back home and settled down in the dining room. Dipping her yellowtail into a small bowl of soy sauce, she made a list.

CLOSING MAGPIE'S

1. Ring accountant re: selling business, net worth, etc.
2. Cancel cleaning service
3. Ring suppliers and cancel orders
4. Review lease
5. Payroll
6. Inventory. Sell furniture? Put in storage?

The room felt thick and airless. Maybe the sushi was bad. Throwing open the window, she breathed deeply then gasped at the sight of Kate and Tony hurrying up the front walk.

"Mom, I see you!"

Cornered, she opened the door. Back at the dining room table, Tony helped himself to her sushi while Kate launched into a diatribe about how worried she was; why hadn't she, Margaret, returned Kate's calls; and did she need a psychiatric evaluation or antidepressants?

My god, Margaret thought, I've raised an American.

"I don't need a mental institution, Katie. I need . . ." What did she need? The list was endless. Reliable help, respect, purpose in life came to mind. But it was overwhelming.

"I daresay you need a holiday," said Tony. "Months and months. Preferably at an old friend's country estate. With horses and servants and a breakfast buffet."

"England," said Margaret, wistfully. "What about the tearoom? I have a lease, I have bills . . . if I'm not making any money, then I'll have to close it."

"I'll pay for it," said Tony gallantly, finishing up the Spicy Tuna Roll. "I'm quite rich at the moment. I landed a series."

"Television? But you detest that sort of thing."

"True! But the beauty of this role is that I don't actually appear on screen. I'm the voice of King Canterbury—a wise and noble puppet. Very plummy accent and all . . . you know how Americans are so easily impressed by that. Anyway, darling, I'm swimming in cash. Not to worry."

Margaret was stunned. To be on the receiving end of Tony's largesse was, well, unexpected.

"For some reason, certainly not of my doing, I'm always cast as the hero."

Something inside her hurt and she looked away. A flood of tears wracked her elegant frame, threatening to snap it.

"Margaret." Tony reached out to touch her shoulder.

"Don't!" She pushed him away. The thought of his caress was unbearable.

He had been everything to her once. They had married at twenty and had been inseparable for two decades. They had worked together, crossed the Atlantic together. Tony was dazzling and she was his partner and it had made them strong enough to forge a life in a new country.

But they were no longer beautiful and young or, in Tony's case, heterosexual. She cried for everything that was gone, for a life left behind and a marriage over. She cried for the sheer agony of being fifty-six and alone and living in Los Angeles.

Kate grew frantic. "Dad! She's freaking out!"

"Kate, please," said Tony, frowning. "Your mother is crying, for god's sake. I can assure you, there's nothing clinically wrong."

Margaret's sobs subsided, then she rose, clutching the back of her chair for support. "I think I shall go lie down," she said in a meek little voice.

"Good idea," said Tony, taking her left arm while jabbing his head at Kate to indicate that she should shore up the other side.

Together, father and daughter steered Margaret back to her bedroom. "Your mother has a perfect right to be gloomy," said Tony when they reached her queen bed with the lavender and white embroidered coverlet. "It's a frightful bore getting old. You have absolutely no idea. Are you cold, Maggie?"

I'm not an invalid, Margaret thought gruffly. But she obediently lay down on top of the duvet and allowed them to cover her up with a soft wool blanket.

Kate bent over and kissed her cheek. "Okay, Mom, you just rest. And don't worry. Daddy and I will help you figure things out."

Tony looked thoughtfully at Margaret, past the sharp crease between her brows, to the long-ago girl he once knew so well.

"Take my offer, Maggie, and let me be your hero," he said hoarsely. "For old times' sake."

Hours later, it was dark outside and Margaret woke to the smell of garlic, butter, and thyme.

The fragrance lured her down the hall and into the kitchen.

Tony was sautéing pork medallions and Kate was whipping potatoes.

"While you were sleeping, Daddy and I made plans."

"London," said Tony.

"Then we'll go see Granny," said Kate.

Margaret felt guilty. "What about your move with Jesse?"

"Jesse's fine," said Kate. "He's not needy like Daddy."

"I'm needy?" Tony removed the cutlets to a platter, then deglazed the pan with a splash of Cognac, scraping up the bits of charred meat and garlic.

Margaret lowered her voice. "You're leaving Michael alone with that yoga god?"

"I'm not going, Mags, I am King Canterbury for the next six months. Catch a few plays in the West End and then give me a report."

"You're afraid of seeing my mother," said Margaret.

"There is that."

"We'll have fun, Mom, just us two. We don't need him."

Her beautiful daughter. How did she get so lucky?

"I never wanted to be the kind of mother that relied on her children . . . her daughter." Margaret was on the verge of tears again.

"And you're not," said Kate. "But can't you be the kind of mother who takes a vacation?"

"All right," said Margaret. She turned to Tony. "Thank you, darling."

Tony finished the sauce with a swirl of cold butter. "Don't thank me, Magpie. Thank the bloody Cartoon Network."

Chapter Twelve

❦

*I*t was only seven-fifteen in the morning and they were fighting over food. Again.

Lilly had cooked buttermilk waffles and Deborah had refused to eat them.

"You're being childish," said Lilly.

"You're being motherish," said Deborah.

Sitting on their bed like a forlorn toddler, Lilly watched Deborah get dressed for work.

"Will you at least come home early tonight so we can go to the movies?"

"I can't, we're working late."

"What kind of a life do we have?" Sullenly, Lilly kicked the bed frame.

"Well, I have a busy life and a job I love. You need to find something you love."

Deborah finished blow-drying her long, layered hair. She grabbed Lilly's hand and led her to their tiny home office in an alcove off the living room.

Switching on the old computer she hit the internet and typed, *Bed and Breakfast employment opportunities.*

The screen filled up with B&B job sites.

"Okay," said Deborah, picking up her black leather carrier bag. "Send out your résumé."

"I can't go work at a B&B," said Lilly.

"You can't hang around the house anymore."

"What if it's out of town?"

Deborah kissed her and departed.

For an hour, Lilly was furious. She headed down the hill to the Silver Lake Bakery and told Lynn, the manager, that her girlfriend was mean and unsympathetic and selfish.

While sipping her latte she idly watched the other unemployed denizens in her neighborhood read the LA *Times* and check their email on laptops.

Bored, she trudged back home and took another look at that B&B page.

There were listings in Arkansas, Illinois, Kentucky, and Michigan.

Nothing close to Los Angeles. Scrolling down she discovered a notice for a weekend seminar. "To B or not to B&B?" Juliet Meyer, Renowned Innkeeper, could help her figure it out, next weekend, at the El Encanto Hotel in Santa Monica.

Whipping out her Visa, she used the handy online application to sign up.

The walls of the El Encanto were beige, the carpet was mauve, and the cushions on the sturdy chairs were teal. Lilly wondered if there was a rule mandating that palette in all hotel conference rooms. She had arrived early and snagged a spot in the front row facing a whiteboard and the speaker's table, also draped in the ubiquitous mauve poly-ester. A large easel featured a black-and-white headshot of Juliet Meyer and a printed schedule of the two-day seminar. Lilly studied the photograph. She hoped Juliet would be as glamorous in person.

Peeking around at her classmates, she noticed one bald-ing man among twenty middle-aged women wearing bright sweaters and nondescript gold necklaces.

Every one of them looks like she owns three cats, Lilly thought glumly.

She perked up with the entrance of her instructor. Juliet Meyer was about sixty with a cap of shiny black hair. In a royal blue silk tunic and tangle of rope pearls, she appeared to be starring in a Noël Coward play.

Assuming center stage she appraised her audience. "Ladies and gentleman," she said, nodding at the lone male participant. "I give you a scenario. Let's say you are the proprietor of the Hollyhock Inn. It's two in the morning and someone is banging on your door. You open it to find a hysterical woman from the Skylark Suite telling you that the truck traffic out on Main Street is keeping her awake. She insists you move her immediately. What do you do?"

"Tell her to fuck off," cracked Lone Man.

The middle-aged cat women frowned disapprovingly.

"You might want to consider another career," Juliet told him briskly.

Lilly raised her hand. "I'd offer her earplugs and a cup of tea and suggest that we look at the reservation schedule in the morning."

"A perfect solution," said Juliet.

Lilly beamed.

At the morning break, Lilly muscled her way through a circle of fawning acolytes and touched Juliet on the arm.

"There's a café on the third floor," she said. "May I buy you some coffee?"

Juliet smiled. "Sure. I'd relish a moment away from all this mauve."

Hidden beneath a canvas umbrella on the terrace, the two women gazed at the Pacific Ocean and chatted about Juliet's career owning B&Bs in Vermont, Washington, and California.

"Where do you live now?" said Lilly.

"Santa Monica. I rented a house near here. I don't know what I want to do next. What about you? Where would you like to live?"

With you, Lilly thought.

Back in class, she tried to focus on the charts, tips, and facts of innkeeping but she was distracted by her teacher. A few times she imagined that Juliet smiled at her in a flirty way.

When the day ended, Lilly hung back until the last cat woman had crept away and then she pounced.

"I thought that if you were alone and you wanted . . ."

"Dinner?" said Juliet.

On the walk over to the Third Street Promenade, Lilly chatted easily about her work in the tearoom and Margaret's recent freak-out.

She sort of left out the part about her girlfriend, Deborah.

On Sunday, the seminar wrapped up with a buffet of typical B&B fare: Spinach Frittata, Maple Roasted Bacon, Sautéed Apples and Dried Cranberries, Gigantic Banana Crunch Muffins, and of course, killer coffee.

Afterwards, Lilly chased the other students away with a proprietary vibe. Then she helped Juliet collect the hand-outs and pack them up into a cardboard box.

Standing close together, their hips brushed slightly, making Lilly shiver.

"Did you feel that?" said Juliet.

"Uhh," Lilly was teetering on the edge of sexual melt-down.

"The spark between us." Juliet pulled her into a deep honeyed kiss. "I feel it, too."

"Ohmygod," breathed Lilly.

"I want you! Right now."

"Here?" Lilly looked dubiously at the mauve carpet.

"No, let's get a room." Juliet purred. "Hotels make me feel so naughty. So clandestine."

You have no idea, thought Lilly.

Upstairs, in 402, Juliet slammed the door, dropped the key-card on the bedside table, and shamelessly stripped off her clothes.

What am I doing? Lilly thought wildly. I have a girl-friend!

But the Juliet/breakfast buffet combo was too strong to resist. Consigning Deborah to a remote psychic planet, Lilly tore off her shirt and joined her new lover on the plush king-size bed.

Time and vigorous exercise had served Juliet well. She was tall and beautiful with long, strong thighs and narrow hips. Her teacup breasts had a delicate sag that seemed to spotlight her garnet-red nipples.

Taking command, she slowly kissed Lilly's neck and belly, traveling down to the sweet spot between her thighs.

"Lilies are so gorgeous in full bloom," she whispered.

Oh man, Lilly thought. Who would believe bed and breakfast could turn into bed and . . .

She forgot what she was thinking.

Chapter Thirteen

It was all quite thrilling.

The Thames, the daffodils, the boutique hotel just down the road from Harrods. The smart European style so refreshing compared to the slutty wardrobes and faux casualness of Angelenos.

"Why don't I live here?" Margaret said to Kate, drinking in the hundreds of years of history framed by blustery clouds. "It's brilliant. They're not tearing down all the lovely buildings like—oh, look! Flower boxes!" She swooned over the charming purple pansies fronting a traditional men's shop.

"You're right. It's totally cool. I think the last time we were here it rained the whole week."

Their hotel room was the size of an elevator but they did have a choice view of a quiet, tree-lined square. The reception desk was staffed by a succession of cheery Australian girls with an intimate knowledge of the local pub scene. The Haverly was timeless and quaint and Margaret preferred it to the five-star hotels featuring gyms and conference centers and frightful prices.

They visited the British Museum and the Tate Modern and shopped on Oxford Street. They studied the Fodor's for new cafés and restaurants. Contemporary London was mad for sushi and celebrity chefs, organic salads and raw-milk cheese.

With the fabulous food, the imperial history, and the multicultural throngs, Margaret felt like she was aboard an episode of *Globe Trekker*. And she loved not having a car. Riding the tube with an eclectic mix of people and walking, walking, everywhere; it was freeing in a way. She was included in something grand. She was part of a world-class city.

On day four, she insisted they find her old flat off King's Road.

"There used to be stained glass ornaments and a painted rainbow over the front door," she said wistfully as they scrutinized the now very tony townhouse. "And the kitchen was tiny—no more than a cupboard, really. We ate at home to save money—lots of potato soup and omelettes."

"Yeah, well, the hippies have gone," said Kate, observing a young mother in gray gabardine with a matching pram roll out the front door.

"It is rather posh, isn't it?" Margaret shook her head

thoughtfully. "Back then everyone was in the theater or making art."

"Hmmm," Kate said absently, opening up her guide-book. "Where shall we go for lunch?"

Margaret was thick in the past, remembering her former flatmates. Kiki, a performance artist, had recited poetry while whipping a rocking horse and Dave, a guitarist, had sold pot on the side to support his band.

"Kiki introduced me to your father. They were doing some experimental theater. Very S&M."

"Mom . . . keep it to yourself."

As Margaret followed her daughter down the bustling streets, she wondered what it would be like to live here again. To walk every morning along the river, to buy scones in Marks & Spencer, to commune with her countrymen.

Kate whisked them into a sleek Japanese restaurant with miles of blond wood and a crowd of people waiting for tables. Margaret smiled at the hungry office workers and turned girlishly to Kate.

"I could move back here, I really could. I don't have to live out the rest of my days in a parched desert devoid of culture and grace."

Kate's brow rose nervously. "Mom, you're starting to freak me out again . . ." She flagged down the harried maître d'. "Two, please!"

A few minutes later they were jammed up against a narrow table along the wall. "I don't think you should do anything rash right now," said Kate. "You're on vacation."

Margaret snapped open her chopsticks. "Well, you're doing something rash. You're moving to New York!"

"I've given that more than four days thought! Jesse and I have been talking about it for six months."

"Well, six months when you're twenty-eight is four days when you're fifty-six."

Their server arrived with two menus and a bowl of edamame.

"What shall we have?" said Margaret.

"London is too far from New York," said Kate.

"Nonsense. London is no further away from New York than Los Angeles." Margaret scrutinized the list and found it extremely odd to be ordering yellowtail in Britain.

"Who knows how long I'll stay there," said Kate. "We're not married or anything."

Margaret felt a pinch in her chest. My daughter's moving away! Grabbing the bowl of soybeans, she calmed herself with a squeeze of the fuzzy green pod.

"I don't know why we're having this absurd conversation," said Margaret. "We're here to enjoy ourselves and have lunch."

"Fine," said Kate.

"Fine," said Margaret.

Afterwards, they buried their differences in favor of Portobello Road. It was Friday and Kate was determined to score some treasure at the open-air flea market.

"Did you know that when I first moved here, I worked at Mary Quant's?" said Margaret, dreamily.

"Why didn't you keep any of that stuff?" said Kate, rummaging through a collection of brass doorknobs. "Vintage is big."

"And my hair was very straight, very geometric. Hours of blow-drying." Margaret smoothed her hair to demonstrate, but her daughter didn't notice. "If your father were here, he'd remember," she said emphatically.

Turning her attention to the crowd and the tidy side streets, she wondered if anyone she knew lived here anymore. Kiki had moved back to Devon and they'd lost touch. And Dave had parlayed his knack for enterprise into some kind of legitimate business—herbal teas? Hemp?

"This stuff is amazing but I think I'm over antiques," said Kate, passing stalls brimming with Art Deco sculpture and ormolu clock sets. "I'm kinda into Asian now. Teak. Temple ruins. Spiritual."

Margaret only dimly heard her daughter, having become fascinated by the number of women passing by clad in veils.

"Oh, look at these cute salt cellars!" Kate seized on a passel of miniature pewter bowls and spoons.

"I thought you were over antiques?"

"This stuff is classic. Goes with anything." Then, picking up a silver toast tray she shrugged. "Why do the English eat cold toast and butter?"

"Why do Americans eat Froot Loops? It's familiar, comfort food. I expect once everyone's tired of sashimi they'll be wanting a tearoom again."

"The only people going to tearooms are the tourists," said Kate, who was now snapping up table linens.

"I rather miss the old places."

"Mother, I need you to focus. We have to buy stuff for Jesse's store."

Margaret became aware of the growing pile of booty in Kate's arms. "How will you get it all home?"

"I was thinking about your suitcases."

Chapter Fourteen

*A*fter a week of gloriously warm spring weather, London had reverted to winter. Having left their umbrellas and coats back at the hotel, mother and daughter were now being soaked by a downpour, and, worse, had just missed the bus heading south to Knightsbridge.

"I'm freezing!" said Kate, who, true to her fair-weather upbringing, was woefully underdressed in a papery cotton T-shirt and turquoise slides.

Leaning into the road, Margaret flagged down a taxicab but a couple sporting natty Burberry raincoats and a palpable air of entitlement jumped inside and sped off.

"Did you see that?" Margaret said hotly. "Lord and Lady Tweed nicked our cab."

"Mom, don't worry. We'll get another one."

"No, we won't," said Margaret, feeling shabby and touristy with her wet stringy hair and soggy running shoes.

Kate scoured her city map. "There's a tube station three blocks from here," she said, taking her mother's arm. "Run!"

They descended into the Underground and were immediately packed in with the rest of London seeking refuge from the rain.

"I sort of miss my Jetta," whispered Kate to her mother, as they watched the flabby man across the aisle dig out his ear wax.

"I know, but when we're home, we sit in traffic, wasting gas," said Margaret, feeling as if she should defend public transportation.

"Sitting in traffic with a latte."

Margaret wouldn't admit it, but she secretly yearned for the comfort of her Volvo, too. And as she inhaled the reek of damp wool clothing and was forced to ponder a myriad of musical tastes from dozens of buzzing headphones, she felt her love affair with mass transit dim a bit.

On their eighth evening, back at their hotel, Kate was lounging in bed in her PJs staring blankly at British reality TV.

"Darling," Margaret said, glancing at her watch. "It's time to dress for the theater."

"Do I have to go?" Kate scooted farther down under the covers.

Margaret became annoyed. "The only reason I got tickets to this bloody musical is because it's at the Shaftesbury."

"I'm too tired."

"It's where your father first did *Hair*."

"So I'll lie here and feel guilty," said Kate, not sounding the least sincere.

Margaret set her teeth. "But what about dinner? We're going to Bombay Palace. You know how much I've longed for their curry."

"I'm sorry. Look, you go, I'll just order take-out."

So Margaret set off alone for the West End and a fairly un-remarkable musical about incest and transsexuals and the afterlife. Really, she thought, was it so difficult to write a memorable song? Relinquishing any further hopes for the show, she canvassed the room.

It was a wonderful old place—saved once or twice from the wrecking ball—and it had changed little from the days of *Hair*, which, of course, had been much much more than a musical; practically a *movement*. Alone in the dark she experienced a violent longing for the passion she had known during that heady time when life was somehow more en-chanting.

When she was more enchanting.

At intermission she decided to flee, being hungry and dispirited and entirely uninterested in the second act.

Outside in the frosty night air, she joined the throngs in the street and allowed herself to be carried along until she reached the corner that used to be Bombay Palace.

It was now a Gap store. She looked right and then left, feeling lost and lonely.

Searching the block, she didn't recognize anything. But just across the road was a trendy bar with gorgeous young faces framed in a glowing picture window.

Kate would fancy that sort of place, she thought, wishing her daughter were here to join her. It looks like one of those gastro pubs.

I must let go of the past for a while, she decided, surrendering to the magnetic pull of Scotch Bar. I shall try a new place. No more endless comparisons, soppy reminiscences. Live in the moment! She pushed inside.

"Margaret Moore?" A woman with shocking red spiky hair was suddenly in her face.

"Pamela Grant?"

"Is that you?" they both shrieked.

The ladies embraced warmly and then Pamela stepped back, scanning Margaret head to toe.

"God, you look marvelous!"

"You, too!"

Pamela seemed especially glamorous in a sparkly velvet camisole and crystal chandelier earrings. Wishing she'd at least pinned a jewel on her beige wool blazer, Margaret cringed at how matronly, how perfectly conventional she must appear. She was teetering on the edge of self-loathing and wardrobe envy, when she noticed Pamela directing a server to a table.

"Is this your place?" said Margaret, wide-eyed and confused.

"God, no! Wouldn't that be something. I'm the Monday

to Friday manager, with weekends off." Pamela led Margaret to a corner table with a chessboard veneer.

"Make yourself comfy, Maggie. I'll be back in a moment and we'll have a chat."

Settling in, Margaret had time to study the room. It was a fantasy English library—the sort of place that Harry Potter and his friends might occupy once they started drinking. Floor to ceiling bookcases, green globe lanterns, and even a billiards table next to a marble fireplace. The crowd was divine and animated with scads of black and hair and bangles.

Pamela returned, squeezing into the padded leather chair across from Margaret. "I've ordered coconut mojitos! All the rage!"

Coconut mojitos! Before Margaret could protest, a seductive elixir was presented by a waiter wearing a red plaid vest that showcased his amazing biceps.

"Kelton, this is my old friend Margaret Moore."

Kelton flashed two dimples before strutting back to the bar.

Pamela grinned naughtily. "There's real perks to this job!" Then, raising her glass she said, "Cheers!"

Margaret took a small sip of her cocktail and found it pleasantly smooth and faintly nutty. I really ought to drink it, she thought. I certainly don't want to be rude.

Pamela slapped the table. "So how long has it been? Twenty-five years?"

"About," said Margaret, suddenly feeling a bit shy. Although she and Pamela had traveled in the same circles, they had never been close friends. "Now go on, tell me what's happened? You're here and . . ."

"You know I was a wretched wardrobe mistress," Pamela jumped right in. "Now, let's be candid—never any good. Despised the actors, detested the directors, they're all monsters, aren't they? I hadn't worked in ages. Then Alan died—did you know? Five years ago? Heart attack, very sudden, runs in the family—and there was no money. No insurance, no savings, I must say it was bleak, Dickensian! Well, I had to get a job, didn't I? The only thing I was ever good at was staying up all night. And really, I adore the theater—just hate working in it—so here I am, every night, with the theater crowd."

Pam replenished herself with a slug of mojito then drew closer to Margaret. "What happened with you and Tony? Heard you two got divorced, must say am not surprised, always thought he was a poofter. But so gorgeous, if it was me, I'd pretend not to notice. Not that you did, of course . . ."

Margaret remembered that it could be quite challenging to get a word in with Pam. Listening to her prattle on, she had time to consider the deep, dark circles under Pam's eyes and the prominent creases in her sturdy forehead. Poor girl, Margaret thought, working nights! That's got to be a hard one. It sort of takes the glamour right out of that saucy camisole.

The second mojito went straight to Margaret's chatterbox and—in between Pam's rages about her cheating husband and lazy children—she found herself revealing that sex with Tony had been mediocre and that she occasionally wondered how life would be different if she had married Sir Malcolm.

"Malcolm's fat as a pig now," said Pamela with relish. "On his third wife. The son's a spectacular drug addict and the daughter still lives at home and knits bird nests into tapestries and says it's art. Men are such rakes, I expect Tony's the same."

Margaret was ready to join the comforting sorority that despised all men but then suddenly, she capitulated.

"No, actually Tony was . . . is a good man. We were just so young, so naive when we married. I expect the acting was everything to him for a long time. It didn't matter much that he had to play it straight until the jobs waned. Then, well . . . it was obvious he couldn't go on pretending. He drives me bonkers but the truth is, I can never stay mad at him."

"Who can?" Pamela was bubbling. "That's his charm!"

"Then of course, there's Kate. My beautiful Kate. She adores her father, warts and all. No, we're rather a happy little family now. Without the sex and the marriage."

Somehow this struck them as unbelievably hilarious and they laughed until their ribs threatened to collapse.

"So," Pamela's eyes sparkled along with her jewelry. "California! Tell me all about it. You're a clever one, Maggie, spending your days in the sun with the movie stars. I do envy you."

"You do?" Suddenly, despite the hateful stretch wool trousers and unassuming loafers, Margaret felt glamorous herself. Even though LA had ceased to be exciting to her, it was rather thrilling to be having a life that someone else coveted.

So, grateful to be the object of curiosity and envy, Margaret closed her eyes, scoured her memory, and attempted to conjure up the names of all the celebrities, no matter how inconsequential, that had crossed the threshold of Magpie's in the past twenty years.

Skewers of meat and bowls of dipping sauces arrived along with a third cocktail and Pamela grew melancholy. "Did you ever think of coming back home?" she said.

For a split second Margaret was thrown by the question and had to think where home was.

"You mean London?" she said. "I'm not sure it was ever really my home. I was only here five years, and"—counting figures in her head—"I've now spent more than half my life away from England."

It was an astounding fact. Or at least, it felt astounding under the three-cocktail circumstances.

By two o'clock, Margaret and Pam had run out of conversation and, promising to write and email and visit, they bid each other goodnight.

Back at the hotel, Margaret made three attempts to swipe her keycard through the slot but the red light held firm. Finally, giving up, she knocked softly.

"Kate? It's Mom."

Stumbling out of bed, her daughter opened the door.

"Sorry," said Margaret. Then she giggled.

Kate's eyes flew wide open. "Mom, have you been drinking?"

"Just a little. Ran into an old friend. She insisted."

"Really?" Kate cracked a smile. "I must remember to send that woman a thank-you note."

It was ten the next morning before mother and daughter awoke and opened the curtains on a dreary gray day. Somehow it felt like an enormous effort to get out of their room, what with pulling on layers and then deciding what to do.

Slumped on the edge of her bed in jeans and her mother's raincoat, Kate yawned and flipped through her Fodor's. "Maybe Charles Dickens's house?"

Margaret sensed a headache brewing. The thought of wandering through a drafty Victorian with an earnest docent was odious. "I think I need to eat something," she said weakly. Squinting at her watch, she realized the hotel dining room was now closed.

"Let's go have a proper English breakfast," she said, rummaging through her quilted toiletry bag for two Advil. "Eggs, bacon, beans, toast, and marmalade."

Twenty minutes later, they were waiting impatiently for coffee in a bustling café near Hyde Park. Kate watched as a dozen other patrons sipped from steaming mugs and dipped their toast into pools of luscious golden egg yolks.

She flagged down a waitress in a black turtleneck and Rasta braids. "Excuse me . . . we've been waiting for our coffee."

"Everyone's waiting for something," Rasta Girl said.

"And no one's taken our food order."

"Haven't they, now?" With the sway of the unhurried, Rasta Girl crossed the floor and joined her fellow server behind the counter. "American Pie thinks she's waited too long," she whispered loudly.

Two pairs of critical eyes rolled loudly in Kate's direction.

Kate's ears grew crimson and she appealed to her mother for backup. "That's not what I said!"

"Indeed," said Margaret. "Those two make Clarissa and Lauren look like Employees of the Year."

"You would never put up with that at Magpie's."

Margaret was about to nod emphatically, but changed her mind. She knew it was difficult to get good help.

Kate continued to froth. "You should talk to the owner . . . they'd listen to you."

"Oh, darling." Margaret's head throbbed. "Not this morning."

"Then we should leave." Kate scraped back her chair.

Despite her blinding headache, Margaret rallied to the cause and joined her daughter in a dignified exit.

"What was with that attitude?" said Kate, marching down the street. "I mean, we waited forever for someone to come over. And we were nice about it."

"Where are we going?" said Margaret, trotting faithfully behind. Her mouth was dry. She wished she had got her coffee before Kate embarked on this protest.

"You must know someplace nearby."

Margaret racked her brain—wasn't there a café on Sloane Square?—but her mind felt cottony and clouded. She must never again drink mojitos.

Ducking under a navy awning, Kate thrust the guidebook at her mother. "Do you want to look through this?"

Margaret perused the entries twice before realizing that the page was blurry and she hadn't read a thing.

Kate's eyes shimmered with tears. "I'm so hungry. I'm sorry I made us leave. I don't know what's wrong with me."

"Darling, you're just overtired. On every holiday, there's a moment when everything falls apart and I suspect that moment is now."

"No, it's not that." Kate twirled her hair contritely. "I feel guilty because I was a total bitch last night and made you go alone."

Margaret reached out and smoothed her daughter's locks. "I'm glad you stayed in. It really was all for the best. Running into Pamela was a happy coincidence. And you would have been bored to tears with all our reminiscing." She kissed the top of Kate's head. "Did I mention the play was dreadful?"

They hugged, and Margaret sighed. "All right, all better. Now, we really must get some coffee before I collapse." Glancing down the road she spied a familiar green sign. "Look, there's a Starbucks. Let's go there."

Kate frowned. "Are you sure? I thought you wanted a proper English breakfast."

Margaret groaned. "I want espresso and the *Guardian* immediately." Then, lacing her arm with Kate's, she steered them towards a grande cappuccino and any coffee cake that was fully glazed.

Chapter Fifteen

*A*bout an hour into class, Clarissa felt herself relax. I know what I'm doing, she thought. I have over twenty years of acting experience from which to draw upon.

This is so natural. I know what I'm doing.

For a week she had prepared for her first students. She'd pored over plays, Xeroxed dozens of pages, and consulted notes from years of study with her own mentors.

The moment the first two actors stood before her, the anonymous classroom became a stage. She and her students were drawn closer together through the magic of performance. Watching the scenes, breaking them down, critiquing the choices came easily.

Afterwards, she was too pumped up to go home. Impulsively, she drove down Franklin to The Company Theater. It was Tuesday night and she knew Vince would just be finishing up with his students.

Waiting outside on Vermont Avenue, she scanned the titles in the adjacent bookstore window until he emerged from the theater. In a ragged suede jacket and faded jeans, he had a laid-back manner that reminded her of a previous era in Los Angeles.

She rushed over. "Vince! Can I buy you a drink?"

He smiled. "Let's go."

Once seated outside at the French bistro, they drank red wine and analyzed years of acting theory.

"I can see where they're faking, not digging deep enough, not trusting," she said. "But what can I do to help?"

"Sometimes just busting them is all they need. Depends on the ego . . . massive or fragile?"

"I really enjoyed myself tonight. It was all the fun of acting without all the bullshit."

Hesitantly, she touched his forearm then lowered her eyes.

"Thank you . . . I didn't think I'd be saying that but . . . it feels good. Being a part of a group of actors."

When she looked up again she noticed his face had turned darker.

"Life hasn't been easy on people like us," he said huskily. "We're talented, knowledgeable. Hard workers. But sometimes, not as fortunate."

She sat quietly. What could she say? It was as if he had opened a door to her innermost self and stepped right in.

Then the easygoing flow returned and he signaled for the check.

"But I want to pay," said Clarissa, opening up her wallet.

"I know," he said, leaving cash on the tray. "Where are you parked?"

They walked back to her car in silence. He wants to kiss me, Clarissa thought.

So she let him.

Pushed up against her Jeep, they had a hot five-minute make-out session.

"You want to come back to my place?" His arms tightened around her hips.

I do but I don't want to spoil this evening with sex, she thought.

"Not yet," she said.

He shrugged good-naturedly. "Had to try."

"It was a good try."

"I'm going to the Taper to see Justin Levy Friday night." He kissed her again. "Want to go?"

"I'd love to."

She jumped into the driver's seat feeling giddy. A Friday night date!

When she arrived home she searched out her vibrator.

She hadn't used it in a long time, but now there was something to think about.

Every day for a week, Lilly slipped over to Santa Monica and cooked a superb lunch for Juliet. Lobster salad with corn and avocado. Fettuccine with fava beans and minted butter. Strawberry panna cotta.

Then they'd spend the rest of the afternoon having sex.

Juliet wanted to hear all about Lilly's life growing up with Cora and then all the stories about Lauren and Clarissa.

"I love your take on life, Lilly," said Juliet as they were lounging in bed, feasting on the last morsels of succulent lobster. "You're straightforward. You cut out the middle-man."

On Friday, they were snuggling under the covers when Juliet suddenly sat up.

"Okay, who is she?"

"Who is who?" Lilly said uneasily.

"Your girlfriend, of course. Don't you think I haven't noticed why we're not at your house? One of the perks of turning sixty is that my bullshit meter is finely tuned."

Lilly pulled the blanket around her as if to cover her shame.

"I wanted to say something . . ."

"Oh, come on, Lilly. For god's sake, I've seen your nooks and crannies!"

Lilly coughed nervously. "Her name is Deborah Fried-man. She's a casting executive, she's married to her work, and she's . . . young."

Juliet waited.

"She's thirty-two," Lilly finished lamely.

"Why, you old slut." Juliet arched a brow. "Cheating on your trophy wife."

"It's not like that. She's always working . . . we hardly ever see each other."

"Then why are you with her?"

If I left, Lilly thought, then I'd be alone.

Juliet jumped off the bed and swooped over to her closet. She pulled out a gold kimono and wrapped it tightly around her waist. "I prefer living alone to living with some-one who doesn't love me."

Is she a mind reader, Lilly thought uneasily. Or am I just obviously pathetic?

"You're right . . . I have no good excuses," Lilly said in a tiny, girlish voice.

"So then . . . what are you going to do about it?"

Driving back to Silver Lake on the 10, Lilly bobbed along in a sea of brake lights creeping towards the downtown interchange. With plenty of time to think, she rehearsed her lines over and over. *I love you but we're not really a couple anymore. It's all my fault. I don't think we can make this work. I love you but we're not in love. I think we should see other people.*

She conjured up all the advice she'd gleaned over the years from self-help best sellers. *Don't stay in a toxic relationship. Don't be an enabler. Don't expect her to change. Don't look to her to make you feel complete.*

The difference between those books and real life, she thought glumly, is that in books you're strong and capable.

Unable to marshal the energy to cook dinner, she picked

up some Pad Thai on Silver Lake Boulevard and then headed up the hill.

Her house was dark and empty and she ate alone in the living room with the TV for company.

About ten o'clock, Deborah came home and Lilly met her at the front door.

"Hi, honey," said Deborah, giving her the briefest kiss on the mouth. "Did you find a job?"

"Sort of," said Lilly, nervously.

"Is there anything to eat? I'm starving." Deborah entered the kitchen and dumped her laptop on the table. Between bites of Lilly's leftovers, she checked her email.

"These noodles are fabulous."

Lilly sat down across from her. "I need to talk to you."

"And I need to talk to you. You know how you're always saying we should go away . . ." Deborah fluttered her feathery lashes and smiled.

Temporarily derailed by hope, Lilly decided not to mention the affair just yet.

". . . we're going to Palm Springs this weekend," Deborah finished, scrolling through her inbox.

"We are?" The image of Deborah lolling around a pool in her blue tankini erased Juliet from her mind. She fantasized about spreading sunscreen over her lover's tawny body, her hand gliding under the slick nylon panty into the wet darkness down, down . . .

". . . then Marcy invited me and I knew I was finally in with her."

Lilly tripped at the mention of Deborah's boss.

"Marcy?"

"Haven't you heard anything I've said? She invited us to her place in the desert."

"You want to go away with me and your boss?"

"This is a huge deal for me. I was hoping you could make your steak with Parmesan and arugula one night for dinner. She'd love that!"

"But I thought it was just the two of us." Lilly felt bruised.

"It's a weekend away." Deborah shrugged. "I thought you'd be happy."

Pop! Lilly's fantasy balloon had burst and she was now definitely back on terra firma.

Before we make any plans, she thought, *I should really tell her about my week in Santa Monica.*

Chapter Sixteen

Heading north from London, Margaret found herself battling twin dragons: first, the rising anxiety about driving on the left and then, worse, an increasing alarm over every new development that, in her view, sullied the virgin countryside forever.

"Look at that!" she said to Kate, gesticulating wildly. "It reminds me of those vile Stepford communities you see on the way to Ojai."

"Mother, that's like, two new homes. And they're nice."

"You mean, they're not as tasteless as Southern California."

Kate rolled her eyes. "Shropshire looks exactly the same to me. Look, same cow, same river, same farmer."

Margaret took a deep breath, hoping to steady herself.

Kate was right. Did she expect the world to remain as it was, forever enshrined inside a snow globe?

Kate, immersed in her iPod, said, "You always get this way around Granny."

"I do not."

Drawing up to her mother's house, Margaret noted peeling paint on the bay windows that flanked the front door. Her critical eye swept over the small dark brick cottage, silently appraising the crumbling walkway, a broken lamp, and ratty boxwood hedges.

"Looks like the gardener hasn't been here in a while," said Kate.

Just as they popped the trunk it began to rain. Hastily, they dragged their luggage along the bumpy path. Kate leaned on the doorbell and Roger began to howl from deep inside the house.

"I can't believe that beagle's still alive," said Kate. "He must be a hundred."

"He's not allowed to go before your grandmother."

Evelyn Throssel opened the door holding her squirming dog. Rigid and unyielding despite her fragile bones, she glanced outside and frowned at the downpour.

"Isn't this weather disgusting?"

Allotting one dry, anorexic kiss each, she then moved aside and let them fend for themselves.

Looking around the house, Margaret was aghast at the cobwebs in the corners and the fur balls clinging to the floorboards. Her mother had always been a fastidious housekeeper.

Well, she was almost eighty, Margaret conceded. Certainly she's earned the right not to keep the house in perfect shape. Besides, who ever visits?

Once their jackets were properly hung in the cloakroom and their suitcases tucked upstairs, all three settled down to tea in the living room.

Nothing's changed, Margaret thought, sipping a weak and unfortunate Darjeeling on the drooping navy sofa. The framed childhood photos of her and her brother James were stationed on the mantelpiece. Aunt Gert's china remained in the cabinet, shut up with a fine layer of dust. The carpet was frayed and smelled dank and doggy, for Roger freely roamed the furniture.

Kate plucked a cookie from the gold-rimmed plate and the beagle sprang up and snapped it out of her hand.

"Granny! He almost bit me."

"Oh, he didn't mean it, did you, Roger, dear?" said Evelyn, offering her spoiled companion her own stale shortbread.

Kate cheerfully filled her grandmother in on life in America. Evelyn tsked once or twice and petted the dog, who was licking the buttery grease off her fingers.

"What happened to the football murderer? Doesn't he live near you?"

"O.J. Simpson?" said Margaret. "He lives in Florida now, I think."

"I don't know how you can stay there. All those killers. That actor who shot his wife."

Kate and Margaret exchanged a bemused look.

"Well, we all carry guns, Granny," said Kate.

At half past five, a young woman from Meals on Wheels delivered Evelyn's dinner.

"I don't cook anymore," Evelyn said grandly.

Not that you ever did, thought Margaret.

"What are *we* going to eat?" said Kate, with the faintest edge of alarm.

"Perhaps you and your mother can go round to the pub."

It was a ten-minute walk to town and The King's Arms. Kate and Margaret were tucked into a burgundy leather booth listening to the din from the television over the bar. They were alone save three middle-aged men drinking pints and quietly watching the soccer match.

"Here's something to take the chill out." A smiling blonde with meaty forearms served up a dose of hospitality along with their dinner.

Now this is old-fashioned English food, thought Margaret, staring down at the soggy steak and kidney pie. Clearly London's culinary revolution had not reached her hometown.

"It's so gross," said Kate, pushing back her plate. "And poor Granny. The house is a mess. Can't she afford a cleaning lady?"

"She would never pay for something like that. Perhaps we could tidy things up while we're here."

After a half hour of picking at their meal, they abandoned the pub and walked down the main street. One by one the chemist and the optician, the baker and the accountant locked their doors and hurried home, past the brick buildings and peaked roofs of Market Drayton.

Trudging up towards Evelyn's house, Margaret enjoyed the smell of clean, fresh air and the familiar stillness of her old neighborhood. A blanket of mist had settled into the dell between the low-lying hills.

"It's so dark out here," said Kate warily. "And super quiet."

"Isn't it?" Margaret said happily. "This is the road Uncle James and I walked to school every day."

"Really? You didn't have carpool?" said Kate.

Margaret laughed. Kate had only known life in a big city, with lots of people and activity. "It was fun, growing up in the country. All the hills and trees were our own little kingdom."

Kate shivered.

Margaret stopped. "You know, moving to a small town will be good for you. You'll experience something completely different."

Her daughter looked shy and fearful. "But what if I hate it?"

"Then you'll make other plans. But really, Kate, you're the perfect age for such an adventure. And you'll be with Jesse. You'll set off together."

"I guess."

"It's wonderful to have someone to share that with."

"Yeah, once I'm there it'll be great," Kate said doubtfully.

That night, lying in her old bedroom on the sagging mattress, Margaret couldn't sleep. The room was ice cold and a bit oily, as if years of cooking grease had lodged in the faded wallpaper. It's not a very pleasant room, she realized; had it been pretty when she was young? Searching her past for fond memories, she remembered looking out the window towards the center of town and dreaming about the cities beyond. There were long-ago friends, and of course Dad. But after a lengthy investigation, she found her childhood utterly boring and dropped off into a heavy traveler's sleep.

Breakfast was always taken in the breakfast room, a cramped nook off the kitchen with a view of the neglected garden. While Margaret and Kate dunked their tea bags, Evelyn squeezed between the table and an enormous sideboard to remove the Diana and Charles commemorative cup from its exalted position on the curio shelf.

"I bought this for you when you were just a wee thing," she said, placing it before Kate.

"You could get a lot for that," said her granddaughter. "Diana memorabilia is big."

"I would never sell it!" Evelyn scowled and withdrew her cup.

"Didn't you say you bought it for me?"

"To use when you're here."

Kate opened her mouth to argue, but a glance from Margaret changed her mind.

While washing up the breakfast dishes, Margaret

wondered idly about her tearoom, whether customers were calling and if Tony had paid the bills on time.

She thought fondly of the beet salad she'd had at June's that night with Lilly and how easy it was to just hop in your car in a sweater and slacks and not have to bundle up for the cold. She was on the verge of speculating about Lilly, when she noticed the dingy gingham curtains over the sink.

Reaching up, she unhooked the metal rod and slipped them off. They really needed a good scrubbing.

After her morning meal, Evelyn always retreated to the sofa to finish the crossword puzzle and watch television. Margaret, feeling cooped up in the house, was determined to get out.

In the cloakroom hung fifty years worth of foul weather gear. Pulling on shabby macs and black rubber boots, Kate and Margaret tromped down the road to the footpath.

For an hour.

Once thoroughly chilled, they returned and sipped tea in the quiet living room with Evelyn.

For an hour.

Then there were twelve more hours to fill.

"You cheated on me!" Deborah shoved her dinner plate across the table, sending it crashing into the dessert platter of sliced melon and mint.

Now I have her attention, Lilly thought sadly. Loathe to discuss the affair on an empty stomach, she had waited till they finished their roasted tomato tarts before mentioning her deception.

"I went to that B&B seminar and we had dinner and . . . it just happened."

"Why would you sleep with an older woman?"

Because the way she's lived her life makes her sexy, Lilly wanted to say. But how could you explain that to someone who's only thirty?

"I can't believe it." Deborah's eyes were hollow and shocked.

She thinks I'm worthless, Lilly thought angrily, because I'm fat and fifty. "Just because you don't want to doesn't mean no one else will."

"So that means it's okay to cheat on me?" Deborah started to cry and Lilly softened a little.

She thought of Juliet, bursting with confidence, standing strong and proud in front of her adoring audience. That's what I want, she realized. I don't want to cling to Deborah because I'm scared.

"I wish I hadn't done it," she said quickly. "It's just . . . you work all the time and it feels like I'm always home alone."

"I have to work all the time if I want to move up. You know that . . . you got me this job."

"But . . . we're not really a couple anymore."

"Did you cook for her?" Deborah sniffled. "Did you make the same things you make for me?"

"Well," said Lilly, uncomfortably. "There were waffles and that rib-eye steak with the Gorgonzola."

"You made her my waffles?"

"But you never eat them."

"That's not the point."

Lilly was beginning to feel curiously detached. Not every breakup is devastating, she thought. We're starting to sound like roommates venting.

"Couldn't you be less needy? Maybe see a therapist?" said Deborah. Nervously, she picked up her cell phone and glanced at the message box.

Wow, Lilly thought, this is truly the most boring breakup I've ever had. "Any important calls?"

Caught, Deborah dropped the phone. "What about this weekend? Just go with me to Palm Springs."

"And pretend we're together? That only happens on sitcoms."

"It might change things for us."

"Change things for you!"

"You don't understand," Deborah said, as if she were addressing a naive intern.

"I think I understand everything. You don't really want to be with me and I've been too afraid to leave."

"I can't deal with this now. I have a breakfast meeting at seven AM." Clutching her phone and laptop like a security blanket, Deborah swept from the room.

Emotionally spent, Lilly remained at the dining room table and rolled a joint, listening to the pointedly dramatic slamming of drawers in their bedroom.

Don't go after her, she told herself stubbornly. Replaying their argument over and over in her mind, she searched for the exact reason they broke up. You always think there's that one thing, that last word . . . but there isn't, she decided. There are a million things, but our hope and our love make us believe they aren't true.

Ten minutes later, the sharp tapping of dagger heels careened her way. Deborah filled the doorway, her neck taut and a tiny blue vein on her forehead pulsing.

"You don't know how furious I am that you slept with that woman."

"You're right, I'm sorry. I was wrong."

"But," Deborah tossed her hair, "I'll give you one last chance to be with me this weekend. Otherwise, we're through."

"How will going to Palm Springs with your boss fix our relationship?"

Deborah's eyes narrowed. "Is that your answer?"

"If we're serious about our relationship, I think we need to stay home and talk. Maybe see a therapist."

"Fine! Then I'm leaving. You and that bitch Juliet can eat your waffles and fuck each other in some pathetic bed and breakfast filled with fat ugly straight people."

Exactly, thought Lilly, taking a deep drag on her sweet and mellow cigarette.

That sounds perfectly wonderful. What the hell took me so long?

Chapter Seventeen

heir third morning in Shropshire was bright
and sunny.

While wrestling cold butter across brittle
toast, Kate dropped her knife with a clatter. "This is impossible."

Margaret handed Kate her own toast and butter, which
she had spent five minutes spreading to perfection. "It's
such a nice day, I was thinking we should go to Chester and
see the Roman ruins."

"Chester," said Evelyn, as if it were worlds away.

Kate brightened. "Granny, come with us. You haven't
been anywhere in three days."

In three decades, Margaret thought.

"All those tourists," said Evelyn shuddering. "And the
traffic. I can't abide the traffic."

"Traffic?" Kate giggled wildly. "Oh my god. Don't go to LA."

"Wouldn't you fancy a day out, Mum?" said Margaret, gazing through the window at the frilly blossoms on an ancient apple tree.

"What do I tell Joanna when she shows up with my meal? Really, Margaret."

"But wouldn't you be happy getting out?" said Kate.

"What makes you think I'm not perfectly happy?" said Evelyn.

"This looks like a fairy tale village," said Kate, marveling at the black and white timber buildings on Eastgate Street. Then her eyes widened. "A Starbucks! Praise the goddess."

While ostensibly a tourist, Margaret was silently considering the economics of Chester's main thoroughfare. "There's three tearooms," she said to herself out loud. "Too much competition for a newcomer."

"You want to move to Chester?" Kate looked alarmed.

Margaret peered down the narrow road with its beguiling shops of local cheeses and handmade crafts. "It is charming here . . . and I'm almost sixty and—well, it's important that I spend my last years somewhere I love."

"Your last years?" Kate's eyes grew worried. "Are you dying or something?"

"No, I'm just . . ." She paused uncertainly.

"Maybe you're having a midlife crisis," said Kate, bolting towards a caramel macchiato.

Margaret followed her daughter past the familiar displays of coffee and its accoutrements. "I am not in crisis, I am a professional woman considering a change."

"Okay," said Kate, stepping into the order line. "But this is what I think: A tearoom in Los Angeles is novel. In England it's same old same old."

Hmmm, Margaret thought, she has a point. But she didn't want to snuff out her fantasies too soon.

Chester wasn't the only town around.

The following days, they combed the lone antiques store and visited Chislehurst Manor, a nearby castle where perfectly normal people donned low-cut blouses and velvet breeches and reenacted medieval England.

"We've pretty much seen all the sights," Margaret said to no one in particular at breakfast on Thursday. She glanced at her watch. The hours looming ahead were crushing her.

"Remember the Quincys?" said Evelyn, biting into her burnt toast.

"Out by Longlands Farm?" said Margaret.

"They moved to Spain last year. Imagine. Living with all those Spaniards."

Margaret considered the bleak and cheerless morning outside. "They probably fancy the weather there."

"I couldn't possibly pick up and live with strangers."

"They'll only be strange for a little while. I think going someplace new is exciting . . . broadening really," Margaret said, shooting an encouraging smile at Kate.

"It's hard to keep the young people in Shropshire. They

grow up and move to the city," said Evelyn with a cluck of disapproval.

"Well, there isn't a whole lot to do here," said Kate. "I mean, if you're not a farmer or something."

"That's precisely what your mother said," Evelyn nodded tartly, "when she moved to London."

Margaret folded her napkin. "Why don't we clean out the attic," she said to Kate, scraping back her chair. "That's something to do here."

Pawing through drawers of scratchy woolen sweaters and plaid trousers, Kate was keenly disappointed.

"Where's the cool 70s stuff?"

"I was out of the house by then, darling."

"Duh. This place is sooooo lonely."

"Lonely?"

"I mean the country's beautiful and everything but . . . it's, I don't know, sad."

"It was good when Dad was alive," said Margaret. She was staring out the small paned window at the impressive collection of garden gnomes in the neighbor's yard. "We'd go on long walks with a packed lunch. He loved to take me to the cinema."

"You aren't making it sound any better."

"I wish you'd known your grandfather. He was funny and sweet. Always joking. He loved hearing about London and Los Angeles. If he hadn't married my mum, he probably would have traveled a bit."

Kate rummaged through a black footlocker. "What's this?"

Margaret stared at a beige leather case with worn gold trim circling the edges. "My keepsake box!"

"It's so fifties," said Kate, handing the small chest to her mother. "What's in it?"

"I can't imagine." Margaret pushed the latch. "It's locked."

Using the tip of a pen, Kate easily rotated the plate until it clicked. "These are easy to open."

"It wasn't like I kept state secrets." Margaret peered inside and found old postcards and a map of Niagara Falls. "From my Aunt Gert," she said fondly. "She was the only person I knew who had been to America."

At the bottom were a slim bundle of envelopes tied up with a green velvet string.

"Love letters?" said Kate excitedly.

"My pen pal," Margaret said in amazement. "From sixth grade. Barbara Alonso. She lived in San Luis Obispo."

Kate pointed to a round red circle on the back of the envelope. "What's that?"

"Sealing wax. It was quite the thing back then."

Margaret opened the first letter. It seemed Barbara had little to say except that she lived near the beach and ate hamburgers.

I wonder what I wrote to her, Margaret mused. Probably something equally banal.

She read through them all—Barbara went to Wilson

Elementary, she had two sisters, her favorite color was magenta—but a line at the bottom of one pink page caught her off guard: *"I'm so glad you want to come to California. You'll love it here in the Golden State. You'll never want to leave."*

Margaret cleared her throat of some phantom debris. How silly of me, she thought. Choking up over a schoolgirl's letter.

"What is it?" said Kate.

"It's nothing."

Kate snatched the paper and studied the girlish cursive.

"This is so freaky! It was your fate to go to California."

"I'm sure it was just coincidence."

"No, Mom! Think about it. If you had stayed, you wouldn't have had me."

"I would have had you somewhere else."

Kate hugged her knees. "Nope. I had to grow up in LA. It's my karma."

Margaret was at a loss against this type of celestial reasoning.

"Plus, I don't really see you here." Kate was folding up the letters and nestling them back in the box. "You're a businesswoman. You have a city life."

"But I never chose that life. It was out of necessity," Margaret protested. "I had to earn money."

"But you could have come back here . . . and you didn't."

"I couldn't come back because I had you, I had to think about your best interests. I couldn't have ripped you from your home, your school chums . . . your father."

"Exactly." Kate nodded solemnly. "Karma."

Margaret shrugged. "All right, perhaps your karma is my . . . inevitable decision. However," she wagged her finger, "please do not mention any of these theories to your grandmother. She thinks we're dotty enough as it is."

"Okay," said Kate, sifting through a trove of old buttons in a cardboard cigar box. "Instead of karma I'll say you consulted a Ouija board."

Gathering up some old clothes, the button box, and a pile of books, they hauled them down two flights of stairs to Evelyn's station in the living room.

"You'll not give away those jumpers!" said Evelyn, sorting through the sweaters. "That's good wool."

"Granny, they're old and itchy. No one's going to wear them."

"They're not to leave."

"Can I keep the buttons?" said Kate. "They're so cool. I'd love to make them into jewelry."

Evelyn's mouth quivered.

"Please?"

After a lengthy and painful inventory, Evelyn declared she'd part with the books and the buttons as long as they were put to good use.

"It's wasteful to throw out perfectly good things."

"If we're done here, I think Kate and I will run to the supermarket," said Margaret.

Touring the produce aisle, Kate absently trailed her hand over the stacks of onions and potatoes. "I would kill for a Trader Joe's right now."

"I adore their guacamole . . . . the kind in the plastic sack," said Margaret, suddenly seized with a craving for tortilla chips.

"And their Thai curry sauce. And the taquitos. And the raspberry vinaigrette."

"Kate! Stop it!" Margaret gasped. She picked up a bunch of carrots, admiring their bright color. "Let's concentrate on what's good here."

"Dairy's definitely better here," nodded Kate.

"Right. Let's fetch some cheese . . . and some clotted cream. We'll make scones. Then for dinner, maybe a beef stew?"

"That's the afternoon entertainment?" Kate appeared as if she'd been sentenced to the gallows.

"Can you think of something else?"

"Rent a DVD?"

Margaret pulled a face. Kate knew perfectly well that Evelyn didn't own a DVD player.

At the dairy case, Margaret was delighted to discover a local goat cheese wrapped up in a bouquet of herbs.

"When I move to the country," said Kate, "I'll have the internet, DVD, satellite . . . whatever it takes to keep me hooked up."

"It would be rather nice to watch a movie with our tea and scones this afternoon," said her mother, plucking a jar of cream.

"Maybe we should buy Granny a DVD player while we're here."

For a moment Margaret considered it. But quickly, reason prevailed.

"She'd never use it. She's perfectly happy with the BBC."

"Yeah, you're right," said Kate. "She doesn't really need that stuff. It's kind of cool, actually . . . living simply."

"That's a rather wise observation." Margaret gazed thoughtfully at her daughter's attire: the snug, tan corduroys with the frayed hems. The black leather messenger bag slung low over her slender hips. "Oh, why would you be excited about baking scones," her voice quivered. "You're not ten years old anymore."

"Mom, don't get all weird," said Kate, giving her mother an affectionate squeeze. "You know I like tea . . . just not every afternoon."

Margaret nodded, then peered down at the cheese and cream in her basket. She placed them back on the shelf. "I don't want tea, either. There's a cinema about thirty minutes away. Let's drive over and see what's playing."

Lauren was sprawled across Dakota's bed, watching reruns and drinking bottled cappuccino.

It had been almost two months since she left Magpie's and she was broke. Vicky had sent her five hundred dollars but that only covered take-out and exercise classes.

She was crashing at his place for lack of any better ideas and he was happy to have her and the attendant availability for more sex.

At four o'clock Dakota arrived home from his day job. Dropping a black canvas computer bag at his desk, he kicked off his suede skate shoes and crossed the loft to greet her in the bedroom space.

"Hey, baby, whatcha been doing?"

"Went to spinning, then had lunch with Kim and Alyssa."

He grinned and tumbled into bed with her. "I'm gonna work for a couple hours, then we can go out, maybe get some tacos?"

Retreating to his computer lair, he dialed some Roxy Music on his iPod and dreamed up a virtual world of heroic vampires battling evil greaser aliens in big-finned spacecraft.

Lauren watched him for a while, then stared absently out the window at the commuter traffic backing up on La Brea.

"I called my agent today," she yelled across the plaintive bleating of Bryan Ferry.

"What did he say?"

"It's dead out there. Shows are on hiatus and people are on vacation. Blah, blah, blah."

"Vacation! Let's go to Baja next week. We could camp at the beach. Sweet!"

The thought of spending more time doing nothing somewhere else was very appealing.

With great effort, Lauren launched herself from the pillows and crept up behind his chair, hugging him from behind.

She admired the graphics on the screen. His world was a tantalizing mix of leather jackets, poodle skirts, and crimson blood.

"I was thinking about getting another job," she said, unconvincingly.

"Only if you want. We're cool for a while."

Lauren smiled. "Really?"

"You'll get something soon." Dakota was relentlessly cheerful, sometimes to the point of creepiness.

"Maybe I should take a class." Her hands wandered from his tight chest down to his lean stomach. "Alyssa was saying that UCLA's summer quarter starts in a couple of weeks."

"What if the Vampires have this whack world under their coffins that looks like the Pottery Barn," said Dakota, glued to his screen.

Lauren gently bit his neck. "It's probably a couple of hundred for a class. I guess I could ask Vicky again."

"I'll pay for it," said Dakota, not looking up from his buxom heroine, Zarina. "And maybe the Vampires could just fuck their victims to death."

"You're so sweet!" She skipped to the bathroom. "I swear I'll book something soon and pay you back."

Peeling off her workout clothes, she flashed briefly on Clarissa who was always taking classes and going on and on about "preparation."

Ducking under the shower spray she thought, maybe Clarissa was right. What the fuck do I know about acting?

Chapter Eighteen

*M*um, you're not ready!"

Evelyn was rooted to the sofa in a blue quilted housecoat.

"James and Natasha are expecting us," Margaret said firmly, buttoning up her short beige jacket.

"Go without me," said her mother, hugging her shoulders. "I feel a bit of a cold coming on."

"But it's a lovely evening . . . and there's a heater in the car." Margaret checked in her purse for the car keys.

"I can't drive at night."

"I'm driving."

Evelyn brushed her beagle's wiry coat. "I won't leave Roger."

Margaret paused, then relented. "We can bring him with us."

"Certainly not! You know Natasha hates him. I simply cannot abide people who hate animals." She bent down and addressed her dog in baby talk. "Isn't that right, Roger Wahger."

"Very well," said Margaret, secretly relieved.

Tall and thin with a crop of nut-brown hair, James Throssel exuded a lightness that immediately put people at ease.

"I can't bear the house now, can you, Maggie?" he said, popping the cork on a bottle of white wine.

Kate and Margaret were admiring Aunt Natasha's new kitchen, with its colorful Italian tile and stylish center island. James filled up four glasses. "Look at the floors! Rotting. And I daresay the attic's filled with rats."

"Filled with crap," said Kate, relishing a large gulp of Chardonnay. "Mom made us clean it. It's like we were nuns doing penance or something."

Natasha had taken great pains to cook what she called "California Cuisine." She gallantly chipped away at a rock-hard avocado for the salad and then removed something resembling enchiladas from her impressive Aga oven.

"I saw it on TV," Natasha gushed, admiring her bubbling Crayola-orange casserole. "It's called Enchilidoes. Festive, isn't it?"

Kate looked glumly at the avocado. "We have this market, Trader Joe's, and they have the most amazing guacamole."

"Oh, dear. I hope the dinner's not too far off the mark," said Natasha anxiously.

"Not at all," said Margaret, giving her sister-in-law an affectionate squeeze. "It looks absolutely splendid."

She threw a critical squint at Kate.

"Don't you agree, Mum should be in a carehome where someone can watch her," James was banging on as they were washing up after dinner.

"She'll never leave," said Margaret, drying a wine glass carefully with a cotton dish towel. "And she's got Joanna looking in once a day."

"If I sold the house, she'd make a tidy sum. Ensure her future."

"Are you speaking as her son . . . or her estate agent?"

He scraped the dishes noisily. "The place is falling apart. The roof, the plumbing. It's an awful lot on me, Maggie. I've got a business to run." He scrubbed the encrusted enchilidoes pan with gusto.

Margaret felt guilty. "Right . . . I'm thousands of miles away. What do you want me to do?"

"Just a little friendly chat. You think she's getting on, she needs more care, all that."

"She won't listen to me," Margaret said. "You're the favorite son. I was never close to her."

"That was bloody ages ago. She's proud of you now, the successful daughter off in America."

"She's never told me that!"

"She's committed to speaking only about the weather," he said wryly, rinsing the pan and then settling it in the dish rack. "Anyway, enough of that. How's Tony?"

"The same as ever . . . funny, charming, maddening."

James peered closely at his sister. "No one to take his place yet?"

"Not yet."

Throwing down his sponge, he wrapped her in a bear hug.

"I expect someone will. Why don't you try that internet dating? I hear it's brilliant."

On Friday, Margaret and Kate tramped down to the Union Canal and forged the footpath along the water.

"Mom, don't be mad but I'm going to change my ticket and leave on Sunday. I thought I could stay longer but . . . I miss Jesse. And, I've got to get back to my real life."

"Right," Margaret said, fighting back a sudden wave of abandonment.

They crossed under a stone bridge and then watched a pair of ducks dive for food. "You could come with me," said Kate hopefully.

Margaret sighed. "I'd feel guilty leaving Granny so soon."

"Really? It doesn't seem like she likes us around."

"She's just very stoic. No whinging, that sort of thing."

"Yeah, she's definitely not the warm cookie-baking type," Kate said thoughtfully. "It must have been hard on you when you were a kid."

Yes, Margaret admitted to herself. But it made her who she was. She wasn't taught to indulge her feelings or surrender to weakness. Her self-reliance had seen her through and she depended upon it.

But still.

She had not wanted to be like her own mother with Kate.

"Don't worry about me. I'm cut from the same tough stock."

"You're not that tough," said her daughter, waving to the owner of a passing longboat. "You're a great mom and I love you."

Margaret rubbed her watery eyes with the back of her hands. "You're just saying that because *you* feel guilty about leaving *your* mother."

"No, I'm just saying that because it's true *and* I feel guilty."

With Kate gone, the house was quiet except for Roger's considerable whining. Margaret and Evelyn ate their cold toast in the morning, watched television, and worked the crossword puzzle.

It rained. Not a hard, abusive rain like Los Angeles but an English drizzle that seemed to creep into the house and pool under the floorboards. The dampness settled in her hair and in her bones and felt like a tiresome house guest who extends their vacation without warning.

To keep busy, Margaret made it her mission to stalk the house, room by room, and give it a proper cleaning. Scrubbing the sinks and washing the dusty china gave her tremendous satisfaction and chipped away the guilt she carried from choosing a life an ocean away from England.

And Evelyn.

In the afternoons, she joined her brother as he drove through the country prowling for new listings.

"Lovely! The perfect village home!" James said one day, as they poked through what James informed her was a quintessential half-timbered English cottage.

"Restore the windows . . . update the heating."

She followed him through a muddy garden into an adjacent stone house. With its blackened fireplace and wavy planked floors, it was easy to imagine a downgraded family from the pages of Austen residing there.

"Captivating," he said.

"If you don't have to cook or clean in here."

"Whoever buys this can afford some help. It's half a million pounds."

"To live out here? Who's going to spend that kind of money?"

"Newly rich Londoners—a few Americans. One can only hope the Shropshire countryside becomes the new Tuscany."

Back on the road, they passed a herd of reddish-brown cows with sweet white faces.

"Herefords. I miss them terribly. Aren't they marvelous? Everything is marvelous. And so beautiful." Margaret rubbed at her throat, feeling that clot inside again.

"Look, we're coming up on the new bridge," said James.

"Aren't you the country squire."

"I am," he grinned. "Never had the wanderlust like you, Maggie."

"And where has it gotten me? I'm just a frightful old hag in Los Angeles. Divorced. Alone."

"Rubbish! You're having tea with all those glamorous movie actors."

"The only actors I know are the silly girls that work for me."

She began to weep and realized, too late, that she couldn't stop. "I'm a bloody failure. I went all the way to America just to pour tea and scrape up after people."

"Christ! Maggie!"

Pulling over, he cut the motor.

"I love the country! I miss Dad."

James sighed. Shifting the car into gear he made a U-turn.

"Right. Well, off we go for a visit."

On the grassy knoll beside his lifelong church lay William Throssel. Kneeling before her father's headstone, Margaret felt a tremendous wave of love.

"I'm glad he's here," she said. "It suits him."

The cemetery was plain and tidy, with weathered graves, an old yew tree, and a low stone wall.

"When I think of home I think of Dad," said Margaret. "Why do you suppose he fancied me and she fancies you?"

"Why does it matter?"

"You're right," she said. "I'm being stupid." She could always admit her weakness to James knowing he didn't judge her.

"I wish we didn't live so far apart," she said.

"Then come back!"

"And do what?"

"Run a tearoom, I suppose. Or, better yet, take care of Mum," he sighed wearily. "I expect she'll be wearing nappies in another week or two."

That evening, Margaret cooked a fine beef stew for dinner and brought up the idea of a carehome.

"James has put you up to this," said Evelyn, peevishly. "Well, you can talk all you want, I'm not leaving my home."

"I didn't think you would," said Margaret. "He is just concerned is all."

Evelyn rose from the table. "They said it will be sunny tomorrow. That would be nice."

True to her mother's forecast, the sun shone brightly on Margaret's walk the next morning. Climbing up on the special rock she used to frequent with her dad, she gazed out over the green hills spotted with trees and clusters of grazing sheep.

"Where shall we go today, Margaret?" he would say, tucking his long arm around her slim, girlish shoulders. "India? China? Timbuktu?"

Strange . . . we never thought of going to America. It had seemed utterly remote back then, and possibly more exotic than the Far East.

Admiring the view, she was grateful for how little things had changed since her childhood. Thank god it hadn't been pockmarked with beastly box stores and hideous development.

If only I could put Shropshire in Los Angeles and surround myself with grass and hills and beauty. Sighing, she conceded her earthly limitations and the sheer folly of thinking that she could possibly have it all.

Not even the kings and queens of England had had it all. Although certainly they tried.

And sometimes, they even lost their heads from the effort.

Chapter Nineteen

∼⌇∽

I couldn't persuade Mum to move," Margaret said to James from her seat on the passenger side.

"You were right," he said dryly, guiding his velvet brown sedan onto the A41. "You have absolutely no influence on her at all."

She noticed they were driving far north. "This seems out of your territory."

"There's a place in Chester I want to show you," he said mysteriously. "Besides, you've got nothing else to do."

At the crossroads of two main streets stood The Cheshire Cat. With its peaked roof and sandstone façade, it looked just like the enchanted cottage in a children's picture book. A handwritten note on the Easter egg blue door said "Closed."

"I have the property description," said James. Reaching into the back seat, he extracted a fact sheet from his cinnamon-colored leather portfolio. "Comes with all the kitchen equipment, dishes, that sort of thing. And two years left on the lease."

"You mean it's for sale?" said Margaret, trembling.

As he led her through the tearoom, Margaret swooned over the leaded picture window; the Delft china and floral tea cozies; the pine green wicker chairs and tables.

She smiled at her brother. Dear James! "It's just the right sort of place, isn't it?"

"The location is brilliant, Maggie. The center of town."

She looked through the glass at a stylish women's boutique, a candle shop, and Kate's beloved Starbucks.

"It is utterly charming," she said. "Why do you suppose they want to sell?"

"Some Londoner bought it on a lark, having no idea that it's a business, not a holiday."

"What about the competition? When Kate and I visited, I noticed quite a few tea shops."

"You little sneak . . . you have been looking!"

"No . . . I mean, yes. Well, I am always curious about other . . . proprietors."

Sitting at a front table, she judged the potential clientele on the street. Tourist season had begun and she noted Germans in sandals and socks; Americans in shorts and running shoes; and Koreans in polo shirts and visors.

It seemed like a flush, jolly crowd. Not dressy, not fashionable, but, thankfully, not demanding and showbizzy.

Could be a relief, really. *From all that*.

If one could order up a tourist's fantasy of a darling English tearoom, one needn't go further than The Cheshire Cat.

And Chester itself was a lovely town. Bustling, delightful, historic, but with all the modern conveniences.

Perfect really.

"No one's made an offer yet," James was prattling on. "We have time to study the figures. As far as the loan . . . there's a couple of chaps I know who'll put you right. What do you suppose you'd get for Magpie's?"

"I have no idea . . . probably more than this place. Third Street has become quite chic, you know."

Margaret felt the thrill of bizarre coincidence. If she wanted to return to England, what better place than Chester? Close to James, close to Mum. A beautiful spot. It seemed as if Lady Luck had stepped from the heavens and extended her hand.

If Kate were here, she'd call it karma, wouldn't she?

James beamed. "It is rather extraordinary, isn't it?"

"Sorry?"

"The listing. The timing. Providential, don't you think?"

Margaret's scalp began to itch and her legs felt jittery.

She stood up and skittered towards the door. "Yes, I must say I am completely overwhelmed! It's . . . quite a proposition. Do you mind if we walk a bit? One cannot . . . make these sorts of commitments on the spot, can one?"

James watched her rattle the doorknob. "Of course not, Maggie. No one is expecting an answer this moment."

Once the idea of buying The Cheshire Cat took hold, Margaret became trapped in a maelstrom of obsession. She drove back to Chester twice to "get a feel for the town." Standing in front of The CC, she allowed herself to dream about it. She pictured small garden tables outside on the street in summer weather. Then she envisioned the savory, steaming meat pies they'd serve in the wintertime.

She grew passionate about the Victorian climbing rose entwined over the blue door. There was something so magical about the place, she could immediately sense its appeal to tourists. Anyone wishing tea in the manner of *Pride and Prejudice* or *Jemima Puddle-Duck* would rush right in.

In her cinematic fantasies, she bought a small house near the shop and rode a bicycle to work—one of those models with a willow basket on the handlebars and a tinkling bell. She'd become jolly friends with the other shopkeepers and would most certainly join a club (dinner? gardening? book?), something she had always meant to do and had never managed in the big city. But of course, in a village things would be different and *she* would be different. Surely the gentlefolk of Chester had oodles of time for hobbies and passions and fulfilling pursuits.

Scoping out the competition was her final task. She quietly dined in the nearby tearooms and was relieved to discover they were no possible threat. One had a dreary view of a government office and seemed almost airless inside; the other served mediocre sandwiches and watery, weak tea.

The Cheshire Cat was far and away the queen of the lot.

Her examination now complete, she concluded, absolutely, that if she were to take the tearoom, she would meet with success. To be sure, it would require an enormous amount of work in the beginning—hiring a staff, cultivating a reputation, nurturing a clientele—but polishing a jewel was her specialty.

Consumed with the pros and cons of selling Magpie's and fleeing Los Angeles, she brewed silently, without a word to Evelyn. Telling herself that it was best not to "get her mother's hopes up," she knew the real reason was that she didn't trust Evelyn to be helpful or understanding with any major decisions in her life.

Why, if she'd waited for Evelyn's approval before running off to London or marrying Tony or moving to California, she might never have left Shropshire at all . . . and then who would she be?

In bed at night, Margaret tensed rigidly against her pillows and dog-eared her list:

THE CHESHIRE CAT

1. Close to James
2. Charming tearoom
3. Tourist town
4. Great location

5. Europe
6. Reconnect to home/countrymen
7. Can age here w/o plastic surgery of any kind

MAGPIE'S

1. Close to Kate? (Only if she returns)
2. Charming tearoom
3. Wealthy clientele
4. Great location
5. America
6. Not allowed to age here
7. Can't think of anything else

She reviewed it again. Of course, the most important thing was to be near her daughter, who was now intending to move to New York. Knowing it was folly to plan her life around a wandering twentysomething, she crossed off *Close to Kate?*

As for charm, both tearooms were lovely in their own way. The CC was a more touristy sort of place while Magpie's required a bit more chic, but she could adjust accordingly. And both enjoyed stellar locations.

But as for the question of the best location, America versus Europe, it was unequivocal: Europe had America beat hands down. As I age, she thought, who would I rather be? A sunbleached hag relegated to the fringes of society, or a woman entering my prime?

One late afternoon, she was reading quietly in the living room, when Evelyn awoke from a catnap.

"James tells me you're thinking about buying a tearoom in Chester."

Fuck all, Margaret thought, pinching her eyebrows together.

"Now don't be cross with your brother," said Evelyn. "You know he could never keep a secret."

"Yes, he did show me a listing," Margaret said in a steady tone. "Quite pretty, actually. The Cheshire Cat."

"Oh. The Cheshire Cat," Evelyn said flatly.

"What do you mean?"

"Chester is not Third Street, I imagine."

"No, but it's lively enough. Lots of tourists, that sort of thing."

Evelyn scratched Roger's ears. "What about Magpie's? Your customers? Katie? Have you thought of all that?"

"I have, Mum. I've been thinking of nothing else, really, the last few days."

Slowly rising from the sofa, Evelyn crept towards the kitchen. "There's a lovely Dundee cake for tea. From Joanna. Shall I slice it?"

Margaret waited quietly in James's office while he finished up a call.

Slouched in a burgundy leather club chair, she swung her leg nervously and surveyed the room. Sales awards and maps of England were framed against blue-striped wallpaper. The simple wooden desk was stacked with papers and books, glossy photos and quarterly reports.

As she admired his profile—the elegant nose and finely etched crinkles around his eyes—she desperately longed to please him, to stay close, to wrap up her life in a beautiful town and tie the bow.

I'm going to say yes, she thought decisively.

He hung up and immediately dialed again. "I'm just ringing Bertie now. He's a whiz at financing."

"Yes." Panic gripped her. "No, stop!"

"No what?"

"I can't take the tearoom."

"Hello?" A cheerful voice bellowed from the phone.

"Bertie? It's James."

"Shall I come round?"

Margaret shook her head childishly. "No!"

"Not yet," said James. "Give us a few minutes, will you? Thanks."

He dropped the receiver with a glower.

"I don't understand. You said you were miserable in LA."

"I was. I am. But I'm not entirely happy here."

"Happiness, Maggie?" Her brother was clearly unimpressed with this line of reasoning. "You sound like you're shopping for a life."

He thinks I've gone daft, she thought. "Being here is lovely, it's brilliant, but somehow . . . it doesn't feel right."

"It doesn't *feel right*?"

Is that what this all comes down to? she thought fool-
ishly. It just doesn't feel right?

"It sounds perfectly silly, but it's the best I can come up
with."

"I don't know why I bothered." Pushing up from his
desk, James stood by the window and stared at the road
below. "It's not like you haven't done this before. When you
left home you said you'd never come back."

"I was a child then. I'm a different person now."

"Are you?"

They remained silent for a moment, avoiding each
other's eyes.

"Try to understand," said Margaret. A sob caught in her
throat. "I can't make a decision like this over one holiday."

James softened. "No, I suppose not."

Returning to his desk, he sorted thoughtfully through a
pile of paperwork and plucked a file marked "Margaret."

"Perhaps we should approach this more slowly," he
said, shrugging into his professional manner. "I think what
I ought to do is email you any listings that might pop up.
We can get a better sense of what's out there—other towns,
other tearooms. You need to make an informed decision."

"Yes," said Margaret. "Yes, that would be lovely."

He glanced at his watch. "I hate to rush things but I do
have business to attend to."

Jumping up, Margaret circled the desk and hugged him.
"I'm sorry I made you go through all this."

"Nonsense. Don't you think I know people change their
minds every day? Par for the course."

Margaret bit her lip. She knew her brother was hurt, but if she said too much, it would only make it worse.

She stepped back. "One last thing . . . I promise I'll come more often. You shouldn't have to care for Mum alone."

"Well, there's a relief."

"I could stay with you and Natasha if you'd like."

"Only if you discourage her from that California cuisine," he said, touching his heart in mock horror. "I had indigestion for two days after those bloody Enchitacos."

They kissed twice—one on each cheek.

Waving her towards the door, he picked up the phone. "Off you go," he said sagely, like a professor addressing a wily pupil. "But mark my words, you'll be back. I saw you weeping over the beauty of the land, I know what it means to you. Don't forget—Americans think nothing of paving over their precious countryside. In another ten years, they won't have any fields left."

On her last pilgrimage on the footpath, Margaret bid goodbye to her special rock and the disinterested sheep. Back at the house, settled in the living room with tea, she watched her mother finish the crossword puzzle.

"The TV says it's going to rain again tomorrow," said Evelyn.

Three weeks and three days, thought Margaret, and we've mostly talked about the weather.

"You're leaving in the morning?" Evelyn glanced inquiringly at her daughter.

"I'm driving to the airport. I'll spend the night there

and catch a plane the next day. You know, Mum, you should come visit. There's lots to see. And," she added pointedly, "the weather is sunny and warm."

"I detest airplanes! They clog up my ears."

Margaret couldn't remember her mother ever traveling anywhere, but she let it go.

"You'll ring when you get home," said Evelyn.

"Of course."

Evelyn put down her pencil and smoothed Roger's neck. "Well, then."

Her suitcase stowed in the trunk of the car, Margaret returned to the sofa to say goodbye. In a puffy powder blue leisure suit, Evelyn looked fragile and Margaret felt a stab of worry.

"Are you ever lonely out here, Mum?"

"Lonely!" said Evelyn. "I have my Roger." She kissed the beagle, who licked her and snuggled in her lap.

Evelyn regarded her daughter sharply. "It's you who's lonely out here, Margaret. Always full of wanderlust, that's what your dad would say. And no regrets, he'd say that, too. Our Maggie has to leave. But our James will stay. He was right, your dad."

Braving her mother's fortress, Margaret wrapped her arms around the thinning shoulders. Evelyn returned the hug briefly, then shook herself free.

"Get on with you, Maggie. I expect your customers will be wanting their tea. You don't want to keep them waiting."

I didn't find a new life, Margaret thought on the flight back to Los Angeles. Or even an old one. She shook her head ruefully. My god! If I am forever dissatisfied it only proves I've become a Yank.

Eleven hours later, when she raised the window shade and glimpsed the unfathomable sprawl of her city, she felt a ripple of excitement.

It wasn't beautiful and it wasn't England, but she supposed it was home.

What was it Kate had said? *I have to get back to my life.*

It was time for her to do the same.

Chapter Twenty

*I*n sunglasses and straw hat, Clarissa was holding court behind a folding table piled with sign-in sheets, UCLA Extension catalogs, and color brochures depicting expressive thespians on stage. The head of the drama department had asked her to chair the booth at the Summer Open House and she was determined to present a polished and professional front.

As would-be actors wandered over, she pitched them with flair and relish. Unquestionably, hers would be a life-changing class and one of the most important dramatic experiences they'd ever have.

They'd better not miss out.

During a morning lull, she tidied up her brochures and then leaned back in her canvas director's chair to scan the crowd. With horror, she spied the figure of Lauren wandering past the Information Desk.

Please, please, Clarissa thought, don't let her see me!

Moments later, Lauren was leaning against the table, hips thrust in a careless pose. Their eyes met.

Fuck, thought Clarissa.

Fuck, thought Lauren.

Clarissa's neck grew hot. All the disappointments of the past year came flooding back, fresh, as if they happened yesterday. Knitting her nerves together, she hid behind her professional demeanor. "Hi, Lauren," she said smoothly. "Can I tell you about our drama classes?"

Lauren rocked back and forth on three-inch platform heels, laced at the ankles with frayed black ribbons. Although striking and beautiful, she exuded a palpable air of aimlessness. Suddenly, it was as if the clouds had parted and Clarissa was peering directly into Lauren's soul: she is brutally insecure! How could I have not seen that?

"You're teaching here?" Lauren wished she had chosen any other class in a part of the city that was far, far away.

"Yes . . . the advanced class. But there are all levels, all ranges. The instructors here are amazing. Our students are doing phenomenal work."

She doesn't think I could do an advanced class, Lauren thought. Bitch.

Surprised, Clarissa realized that she might be over Lauren. And she even felt the tiniest bit sorry for her. She'll never be a good actress and she doesn't seem to care. If it were me, I'd be devastated if I was terrible.

I am a great actress, Clarissa acknowledged silently. And I love the work. I'm not beautiful like she is but now, at my age, it kind of doesn't matter.

Still, she added wistfully, if I had looked like that when I was young, I could have really worked it.

With unexpected magnanimity, Clarissa emerged from behind the table and drew Lauren aside.

"I know we didn't part in a good way," she whispered. "But please don't let that . . . inform your decision. I could find you a really good class."

Is she crazy? Lauren wondered. She heard Vicky's voice say, "Women are your worst enemies."

She picked up a brochure and flipped through it. The actors in the pictures looked serious—like they were saying words from plays or something. God, what if they made her do something hard like Shakespeare?

"Our classes prepare you for auditions and the work," Clarissa was saying. "We tape our scenes and then we review, refining the choices."

She's so big on "the work" Lauren thought. It makes it sound so hard.

Opening the catalog, Clarissa circled two columns with a red felt tip pen.

"You'd love either of these teachers. And listen, you can come the first night and sit in. If you don't like the class, you can drop it."

"When are they?" Lauren asked, teasing up her hair.

"One meets Tuesday and Thursday nights, seven to ten, and the other's Monday and Wednesday."

"I'll think about it," said Lauren, stuffing the brochure in her sequined tote. "Have you heard anything about Magpie's?"

"No," Clarissa giggled, relieved to be sprung from the competitive arena of acting. "I wonder if Margaret's back from her breakdown."

"It's too bad the tearoom's closed," said Lauren. "Now I know it was an easy gig."

Clarissa nodded as if working side by side with this gorgeous creature had ever been easy.

"I don't know about class," Lauren said. "I'm kinda busy. I moved in with Dakota."

"Really?" said Clarissa.

"Yeah. And I'm helping him set up his own company. You know, making business cards and looking for a space. I might be his office manager."

Clarissa offered up a silent prayer for Dakota and his fledgling enterprise.

"Well, good luck, whatever you decide," she said.

As Lauren drifted away, Clarissa thought, that wasn't so bad. I'm in a totally different place. I'm really quite strong. I could probably even work with her if I had to.

As long as no one uttered the word *audition*.

On the drive back to the loft, Lauren pondered acting class. Three hours! That was way long. And Monday nights they always bowled at Lucky Strikes with Dakota's techie friends.

Sitting in bumper-to-bumper traffic on Sunset, she

spotted The Coffee Bean and decided to bail, pulling a sharp left in front of oncoming traffic.

I hope I'm not like Clarissa in twenty years, she thought as she waited for her frothy drink. Alone and wrinkled . . . not even Botoxed. Snapping up a nonfat mocha frappuccino, she hopped back in the car for the crawl home.

And if I signed up for something next week, I couldn't go to Baja. There were a million workshops, she rationalized, but she'd never been to Mexico. So with no further thoughts on the subject, she happily consigned acting class to the hazy, distant future.

Margaret felt giddy on the drive over to Magpie's. Opening the back door, she wandered through her tearoom with trepidation only to discover that in her absence, it had remained exactly the same. Here was the china neatly stacked on the sideboard; the tables and chairs were just as she'd left them. She switched on the fireplace and the flames curled right up.

Fixed with a cup of Lady Grey, she nestled down next to the fire. It felt cozy and familiar but then again, something did nag. What was it? Sipping her tea, surrounded by her familiar things, she suddenly wished it were different. Having returned a somewhat changed sort of person, she was secretly hoping that Magpie's had changed, too.

How utterly preposterous, she shrugged. What am I thinking? That while she was on holiday, the room had magically transformed itself into, what, a wine bar? A day spa? I'm mad as a hatter. There were calls to return, and bills to pay (naturally Tony would have been spotty about that) and cleaning and dusting and . . .

With a second cup of tea, she approached her writing desk and confronted the messages on the answering machine.

"Margaret? This is Susan Tsing. God, I hope you're not thinking of closing forever . . ."

The sound of Susan's voice made her smile. What a lovely cardiologist! And such a stunning collection of shoes.

"Please reopen soon," said the droll Madelyn Cummings. "With you closed, how can I escape from my horrible children?"

"We miss you!" Annette Kline had been her customer for ten years. My best tipper, Margaret thought, underlining the message with flourish.

"You're all I have left in this fucking insane city, excuse my bad language . . ."

She paused briefly; she hadn't expected such anguish, such devotion!

Thirty messages later, Margaret felt humbled by the adulation of her clientele.

How could I have possibly imagined closing my business? she wondered. All these ladies counting on me even if it's only for an afternoon cup of tea! Where would they go if I shut up shop? Their birthdays, their baby showers. A precious hour with a dear friend, or sister . . . or mother.

I'm rather like a public service, she decided. For indeed, who would want to spend life's important moments in a dreary mall, or, worse, a wretched food court? Who could make crucial decisions in a harshly lit room with dozens of cell phones shrieking?

Margaret felt strong and noble.

Her purpose was clear. Magpie's would carry on. Indeed, it would be uncaring and selfish of her to call it quits.

The shrill ringing of the phone broke into her reverie. Snatching it up, she heard the anxious whisper of a Mrs. Robman.

"Hello, Magpie's? Are you back? I didn't know what I was going to do if you closed for good! I'm throwing a baby shower for my daughter-in-law and I need the whole room. You're the best High Tea in town."

"Of course! How lovely!" Margaret beamed. *The best High Tea in town.*

The abrupt realization that she was unprepared to furnish a party of any kind cut through her glow.

"I have just returned from England," she said smoothly, "and I am catching up on business. Please give me your dates and I'll ring you back."

She dropped the phone on the message pad. What was she to do? She was in no position to present tea—there was no staff.

Pacing over to the front windows, she peered down the street. Pretty women in colorful mules dashed to business lunches; speedy valets collected polished cars outside the Italian restaurant; busboys cleared dishes from sidewalk tables.

There is a world of workers out there, she decided. Not to worry. I shall place an ad. Conduct interviews. Call the cooking school and have them put up a notice for a chef's position.

She thought of Lilly.

A twinge of guilt poked her. I behaved appallingly, she thought.

Zipping to her Rolodex, she found Lilly's card. Scrolling further, she found Clarissa, and, finally, Lauren.

Sighing, she swallowed the last drop of tepid tea. She'd better steep a third cup. There was a lot of work to do.

Chapter Twenty-One

 asn't anyone noticed I'm drinking bubbly water?" said Tony, raising his wine glass and grandly swirling the ice cubes.

It was a warm June evening and the family had assembled on Margaret's back porch for dinner. Kate was manning the grill and Margaret was laying the table with the flea market linens from London.

"Daddy, that's wonderful," said Kate, exchanging dubious glances with her mother.

"I haven't had a real drink in a month. Michael's got me on some detox diet . . . you know how those yoga people are." Tony pulled a face.

Margaret felt a trifle put out in spite of her hope that he might have finally reformed. "How on earth did Michael succeed where we have failed all these years?"

"Do you really want to know?" He grinned slyly.

"No," said Kate, brushing the skinless chicken fillets with a honey-mustard marinade. "He's right. You shouldn't drink so much. It's better when you don't."

There was a moment of awkward silence as Tony, lost for a quip or a witty rejoinder, fell silent.

"Darling, has it been hard on you?"

He shrugged philosophically. "This is the price one pays for staying au courant. Abstinence is the new heroin, you know."

Margaret kissed him firmly on the cheek. "Right."

Abandoning the barbecue, Kate plopped down next to her mother. "I have big news, too. I'm not going to New York."

"What happened?" said Margaret, attempting to remain calm while secretly pleased that her daughter wasn't leaving.

"It was all my doing," said Tony. "I told her, 'Look what happened to your mother when she followed a man across a continent.'"

"Daddy, stop it! I decided for myself." Kate rapped her father lightly on his knuckles.

Margaret frowned and reached for the olive tray. "Did you and Jesse have a fight?"

"Sort of. I just realized I was spending too much time helping him with his business. And we're not even married."

Margaret resisted the urge to point out that those were the exact same reasons Kate had invoked when deciding to go in the first place.

"I suspect there's someone else," said her father, deliciously.

Kate looked embarrassed.

"Aha!" Tony clapped his hands triumphantly. "Darling Kate . . . you didn't get the acting gene."

"You cheated on Jesse?" Margaret shifted immediately from happiness to dismay.

"No! Not cheat, cheat. All I had was dinner. At this wine bar on Hillhurst."

Margaret softened. "So this, other person . . . what does he do?"

"He's a doctor . . ."

How thrilling! Not an actor or an artist or a decorator.

"Where on earth did you meet a doctor?" Tony muttered. "I've never met a doctor in my life!"

"At an AIDS benefit. He was at my table. He was wearing a gray suit," she said dreamily, "and a tie."

Margaret smelled something burning. Jumping up, she stabbed the sizzling medallions with a fork and nestled them on a platter lined with fresh rosemary sprigs.

"Are you quite sure about this?" she said. "You were madly in love with Jesse two weeks ago."

"I wasn't in love with Jesse; I was in love with his life," said Kate, happily relinquishing the grilling to her mother.

"I don't quite follow," said her mother.

"I want to have my own shop . . . do my own design work. Jesse made me see that."

"I hope you didn't break his heart."

"Good god, Margaret. These things happen. Romance is temporary," said Tony. "Not like a really fantastic armoire."

Setting the platter on the table, Margaret picked up two serving spoons and tossed the green salad. "So you think it's serious with . . . ?"

"With Daniel? That's his name, Dr. Daniel Geffner. Well . . . we have seen each other every day since we met . . . Mom, the corn!" Jumping up, she ran to the kitchen.

Her parents traded arched eyebrows.

"I rather liked Jesse," said Margaret sadly.

"I don't know," said Tony, slicing into a juicy piece of chicken. "All that decorating, that cooking. Seems a bit suspect."

"Jesse was definitely not gay," said Kate, returning with a bowl of steaming corncobs. "Anyway . . . Daniel is different. He saves people's lives."

"A bloody do-gooder? How perfectly tiresome. But speaking of eligible straight men . . ." He turned to Margaret. "I don't suppose you met anyone on your trip?"

"Me?" Margaret was surprised. "If I did I wouldn't tell you."

"But I'm the gay best friend," said Tony.

"You're not my gay best friend."

"Mom, Dad." Kate issued a warning.

Tony forged ahead. "I met this chap Simon who would be perfect for you. Sixtyish, English, handsome—not as handsome as me—loves to visit the motherland, all that. He's a student of Michael's."

"He lives in Ojai?" Kate snorted.

"Quite brilliant, actually," said her father, twirling a fork-ful of field greens. "You see each other on the weekends and have your weekdays to yourself."

Margaret was enjoying her dinner, her family, and the balmy evening so much she dismissed him easily. "Is it my turn to share some news?"

"That you're going to reopen the tearoom?" said Kate matter of factly.

"How did you know?" Margaret's sails sagged.

Tony shuddered. "Darling, what else would you do? Live with Evelyn? Retire to the country?"

Margaret gave her plate a tiny shove. The thrill she had felt about her own self-revelation ebbed away. "Am I so cli-ché, so banal, so utterly predictable?"

"Is this a parlor game?" said Tony.

Kate felt a tang of guilt. "Mom, ignore him. We want to hear all about it."

Margaret sat there stonily. Really!

"Mom, please. We love you!"

"And we certainly don't want you to go back to England," said Tony. "Unthinkable."

Succumbing to their coaxing, Margaret relented. "I do, in fact, think this city needs me, or rather, the tearoom."

"Of course it does." Kate nodded.

"Right," said Tony. "And while we're on the subject of Magpie's, I noticed you still have those portraits of the Clumber spaniels."

"I would love to get rid of them," said Kate.

Margaret dropped her knife in surrender. Clearly, if she ever hoped to remain the center of attention she'd have to pay a therapist or ring up a good friend.

"It's too much Daddy's taste. You know, merry old England."

"Why don't you just run a stake through my heart?" said her father.

"Magpie's needs a makeover," Kate said excitedly. "Mom, let me make some changes."

Taking a moment to consider this, Margaret skillfully buttered an ear of sweet white corn.

Tony reclined in his wicker throne. "If it didn't look so matronly, you could pull in all the gay boys."

"It's not matronly!" said Margaret.

"I could throw a party . . . invite Simon."

"You can't bring a straight man to Magpie's," said Kate. "That'll freak him completely."

"Let's have a look, then," said Tony, helping himself to more bubbly water. "After dinner, we'll all go round."

Kate was off and planning. After roaming Magpie's for half an hour, she decided that the thing to do was to open up the room with French doors leading out to a bank of sidewalk tables.

"Mom, you're on a great street. Embrace it."

Margaret flashed suddenly on The Cheshire Cat. "You're right. And some sort of old-fashioned climbing rose would be lovely, don't you think?"

Tony was poking through the cups and cozies on the gift shelves next to the front door. He held up a commemorative Silver Jubilee plate. "Do people still buy this shit?"

Consumed by a heady combo of excitement and fear, Margaret ignored him and queried Kate. "What will the old customers think? I don't want to upset them."

"They'll love it. It'll be Magpie's but fresh and bright."

Margaret agreed. We could all use a little freshening—let my daughter have a go at it.

Kate scrutinized the windows. "Do you have a tape measure?"

Turning around, Margaret caught Tony removing the portraits of the spaniels.

"These will be stunning up in Ojai," he said. "Give it the air of a baronial manor."

"You can't have my dogs!"

"They're frightfully tired here. I should think you'd fancy a mirror . . . or a nude."

Trotting behind on Margaret's heels, Tony followed her into the kitchen and watched as she rummaged through a plastic toolbox.

"You will go out with Simon?"

Plucking the tape measure she looked up at him warily. "Why are you banging on about this?"

"What do you mean?"

"This sudden interest in my romantic life."

Examining a cake platter, Tony shifted his weight uncomfortably.

"Christ, Maggie. If you don't get married again, then I shall continue to feel somehow responsible for your unhappiness."

"I'm not unhappy!"

"But there's still . . . something, isn't there? Something hard between us."

"Nonsense." Margaret was shaking slightly.

Tony paced the tiny kitchen, back and forth between the sink and the baker's rack. "Well, then, forgive me. I'm sorry for what happened . . . for being such a bloody wanker. Don't you see . . . I love you very much . . ." Faltering, he grabbed the tape measure from her hands and bolted from the room.

"Tony!"

Reluctantly, he spun around.

For a moment, Margaret reflected on the unsatisfactory nature of apologies. Why is it that when someone finally admits they're sorry, it's not as gratifying as you'd hoped. It doesn't necessarily clear the slate or make you feel better in any way.

There had been many nights he'd made her miserable. But now she traveled back to the last one.

It was an unbearably hot September and she was lying on the couch in the living room, windows thrown open, desperate for a breeze and the sound of his car in the driveway.

When he had finally crept in they fought. She didn't remember everything they said, only that, when the shouting ceased, they'd wept together.

For Tony never denied anything.

"I don't know why I did it . . . it meant nothing."

"Who was it?" she'd begged. "You have to tell me or I'll simply go mad."

"It doesn't matter."

"It does!"

"It's over."

"Not to me."

"A day player. You don't know . . . them."

Bewitched by unsavory forces, Margaret charged to the kitchen and, tearing through a basket of papers by the phone, seized the cast list. Returning to the living room she waved it in his face.

"I will come to the set! I will find her." She began to read. "Carol Simmons? Susan Finley? Rachel . . ."

"Enough!" Snatching the sheet from her hands he said, "Alan Warner."

She surrendered into the armchair. What ammunition could she employ to battle this? There had been men in London but she'd told herself it was the times. Experimentation, the sexual revolution. Everyone was sleeping with everyone else. Even she, Margaret Throssel, had enjoyed a threesome with Tony and that luscious Colin, some faraway weekend in Sussex when she'd been all of nineteen years old.

But after they moved here, after Kate . . . their lovemaking dwindled. She blamed it on the baby, her fatigue, the pressures of the business, marriage, boredom.

She blamed it on herself. If only she were glamorous enough, beautiful enough, sexy enough.

"It won't happen again," he'd promised, falling on her neck, clasping her hands. She knew it wasn't true and that he was a fine actor.

It will happen again, she thought.

But after that night, she decided that when it happened again, it was going to happen without her.

Back in the present, she sought his dusty, sapphire blue eyes. She loved him. She loved him and he had wounded her deeply. But the thing was . . . she also knew that Tony had never wanted to hurt her. He had, over the years, tried to apologize. Yet she had pushed him back, harboring a poisonous venom to keep her safe from his powerful charm.

But now, this moment, she longed to let it go. She no longer wanted him for sex and didn't need him as a husband. She knew that he loved her and he would always love her—certainly as much as Tony Moore could love anyone, male or female. He even wanted to make it right. He wanted her forgiveness. Tony was . . . what? Brilliant and intoxicating and deeply, deeply seductive . . . but not the man anyone should marry.

"Tony," she said softly. "Please, not another word. I adore you and I promise all is forgiven."

Bending down he kissed her gently on the cheek. "I'm so glad," he whispered.

Sweeping out the room, his trained voice carried back to her from the hallway.

"Don't worry, darling . . . I shall take excellent care of the Clumbers."

Chapter Twenty-Two

*C*larissa and Vince were dining at the outdoor café at the Music Center. It was a silky night and a string quartet was having a go at Mozart.

The penne with tomatoes and basil was for her and the meat loaf with wild mushroom sauce was for him. It was their third Friday night theater date and Clarissa was impressed with Vince's status in this world. Their meal was constantly being interrupted by actors and directors stopping by to say hello and gossip about New York or Williamstown; who was cast, who was directing.

Through Vince, Clarissa had reconnected to the Theater—that small band of ragamuffins residing in a parallel universe alongside their famous film brethren. Vince's crowd was either in rehearsal, back from some playwright's festival, or off to Manhattan. They were also fiercely competitive, but Clarissa felt like she was on sure footing with this tribe; that the auditioning game was somewhat meritorious. Sure, celebrities were still offered the plum roles, but not all of them. Plus, it was exciting to be included in the inner circle . . . and to be there with Vince.

His power turned her on. After the show, they had had a twenty-minute make-out session in his car in the underground garage.

"Let's go back to my place," she said, panting softly.

"I'm not waiting another minute to have you," he said, deftly unhooking her bra. "What about right here?"

Clarissa experienced a sharp thrill at the risk of doing it in a public place. She climbed into the back seat while twirling her tongue in his mouth.

Once entangled on the leather bench, her passion was put to the test. With her legs scrunched up around her waist and his left knee jammed into her right thigh she lost momentum.

Most tragically, there was simply no room for oral pleasures and before she was juicy, he was coming.

"I'm sorry," he said. "You're so sexy."

Although pleased to be the object of desire, Clarissa wished they'd gone back to her place. With candlelight and wine, she could have stretched out on the bed and really enjoyed herself.

Vince had a very sweet, apologetic look on his face that touched her and kept an ember burning.

"I always remember teen car sex as so hot," she giggled. "Maybe grown-up sex in your own bedroom is hotter."

"Maybe we should drive there and find out."

They raced back to Laurel Canyon. With two glasses of Cabernet, scented vanilla candles, and Sarah Vaughan, they did it again, slower and deeper. As a consummate performer, Vince could easily play two shows in one night.

No problem.

Afterwards, lying in bed, she was anxious about waking up with him in the morning. Would it feel weird and awkward? Bill, her married lover, had never stayed the night. And even though she was comfortable with Vince, she didn't yet feel that easy intimacy lovers shared.

He, however, was out cold, clearly at home in her cotton handkerchief sheets.

It was novel and unexpected having a man in the house, and she felt restless. Slipping out of bed, she drifted to the overstuffed chair in the living room. Through the picture window, she watched a few cars climbing up Lookout Mountain and wondered where they'd been out so late. She was glad she hadn't slept with Vince right away. Glad that they had other things going on besides sex.

Maybe this is what it means to have a partnership, she realized. She'd had lovers, she'd had boyfriends, but she really hadn't experienced much friendship with men.

By three AM, the newness of Vince had subsided and she crept back to bed. With his warm body acting like a soothing tonic, she soon fell into a comfortable sleep.

Vince was very well trained. About seven o'clock he got up and made coffee, returning with a steaming mug that he placed on her side of the bed.

"Hi," he said.

"Hi," she smiled shyly.

"I was going to make you breakfast, but all I found was soymilk and cereal."

"That's breakfast," said Clarissa.

"Tomorrow morning, at my place . . . eggs, toast, bacon. Real food."

So, there'd be a tomorrow, she thought. It made her feel more secure.

A half hour later, they sat at the kitchen table reading the LA *Times* with bowls of tasteless whole grain twigs.

"I'm doing a revival of *A Streetcar Named Desire*," said Vince. "And I want you to play Blanche. You'd be great in that role."

She laughed. "You mean I had to sleep with you to get the part?"

Smiling impishly, he returned to the Calendar section.

Wow, Clarissa thought, I've never slept with anyone and gotten a part before. Look what I've been missing.

Playfully, she tapped his paper. "You know I've pretty much trained all my life for that part."

His brown eyes looked at her intensely across the table.

"It's your time. You're the perfect age."

No, Clarissa thought. Things are never perfect.

But she wasn't going to argue with her director.

Lilly loved the Sunday Farmer's Market in spite of the taw-dry balloon man with rotten teeth and the Peruvian folk musicians who had somehow become ubiquitous at all out-door events these days.

With her lover in tow, she was determined to find the sweetest peaches and that guy with the big fat mulberries. Quickly bored by the farm stands, Juliet ditched her to graze through the food vendors.

Filling the pushcart with ripe local fruit, Lilly imagined all the possibilities: deep-dish peach pie, Santa Rosa plum tart, summer berry cake with crème fraîche. Sometimes she really missed the tearoom and the hours she spent with her hands in butter and flour, shaping and primping the dough.

Margaret was also headed to the farm stands in search of a real-tasting strawberry—not like the flavorless red golf balls you found at the supermarkets. After circling Vine Street and Cahuenga three times, she had finally nailed a parking spot. Pushing past what seemed like an ocean of whining toddlers in strollers and their chatting, inattentive parents, the last vestiges of her post-holiday rapture with life in LA disappeared.

Why are people having the most intimate conversations in such a public place? she thought. Can't they focus on the fruits and vegetables? She felt like a salmon, swimming her way up Ivar towards Larry's Berries. Squeezing past the woman with the iguana on her shoulder and the gaggle of tattooed hipsters next to the vegan muffin lady, she arrived at the most delicious strawberries in the city. Reaching out to score a three-pack, she came shoulder to shoulder with Lilly.

"I don't believe it!" She gave her former chef a gentle, restrained hug.

Margaret looks healthy and relaxed, thought Lilly. That breakdown must be working for her. "How are you?" she said. "I mean, are you okay?"

"Quite. I spent a couple of months in England. Saw the family and all that."

Lilly had no idea what "all that" meant but assumed it was British for "met my obligations."

"I didn't expect to run into you, but it's rather providential."

"Why?"

"I've decided to reopen the tearoom. And may I be candid?"

"Sure."

"I'm hoping I can lure you back."

"Hmmm." Lilly hesitated. She was having a lot of fun hanging out with Juliet. Returning to her life on 3rd, dealing with Lauren and Clarissa, well, that was a downer.

"You're a wonderful chef, Lilly. And I want to try some new things at Magpie's," Margaret was forging on, despite the crush of aggressive shoppers angling for the berries behind her. "I'm tarting it up. Changing things round. We're adding French doors and outside tables. Kate's idea."

Lilly's interest was piqued. She had always liked Kate and approved of her influence on Margaret. "It feels like . . . years since I thought about tea," she said.

Taking Lilly's arm, Margaret steered her away from the fruit stand over to a small patch of shade under a crepe myrtle tree.

"I've been completely stupid about the menu. Too adamant about tradition . . ."

Lilly eyed Margaret warily. What had happened to her in London? Had her mother died?

". . . Magpie's should be exciting and clever. Embrace the new with the old. Like those mango sandwiches you whipped up. I think they would be quite brilliant."

"Really?" Lilly melted. She had always been a little awed by Margaret's presence and strength. She knew that her former employer thought things through and never did anything casually.

She was on the verge of acceptance when a commanding voice inside her said, Be bold! If Juliet has taught you anything, it's to go after what you really want.

"If I were to come back," Lilly said, "I'd need creative freedom in the kitchen. I can't do the same old thing all the time."

"Right," said Margaret.

"I just . . . don't want to limit myself to making grandmother's scones every single day. I need to explore . . . I need to experiment with different recipes. Use the incredible produce and chocolate and spices we have in this city."

Margaret drew a sharp breath. "You are an artist, Lilly. I appreciate that. And I'm prepared to give you . . . freedom in the kitchen . . . but I do pride myself on good instincts and I would hope that my experience would carry some weight . . ." She hesitated.

"Because it's your tearoom?"

Margaret exhaled. "Well . . . yes."

"Oh, all right," Lilly said playfully. "You can still be the boss."

"Then it's settled . . . you'll have your creative freedom but I'll have . . . suggestions."

"There is one other thing," said Lilly.

"What's that?"

"Clarissa and Lauren."

Margaret nodded her head vigorously. "They won't be coming back. As a matter of fact, I have someone else in mind. Remember Stephanie, the produce coordinator? Turns out she's looking to make a change. And she has all sorts of cousins she says would love to work in a tearoom. Imagine! A whole new labor pool."

Lilly felt hopeful. Maybe this could work the second time around . . . and be something she really wanted to do.

"Could you tolerate your former co-workers for one last tea party?" Margaret said.

"If I don't have to work with them, they're probably all right."

"Then come round next Saturday. Three o'clock. I'll prepare the tea." She smiled at her chef. "You look good, Lilly. Happy, I'd say."

"I met someone . . ." Lilly began excitedly, but was drowned out by the clapping and stamping of the Peruvian pipers.

"I'll call you this week," Lilly yelled. "We'll talk."

Satisfied and happy with this new arrangement, Margaret secured a three-pack of Chandler berries and then pressed on to the choice peach stand near Hollywood Boulevard.

Juliet appeared, offering Lilly a paper plate of warm corn tamales drizzled with Mexican cream.

"Who were you talking to?"

"Margaret. I just got my job back."

"Fantastic. It's time for you to get out of the house."

Lilly felt deflated, like a girl whose birthday party had just ended. "I thought we were having fun. Enjoying life."

"We are. It's been a fabulous holiday. But now we've got to think about our real life. If we move in together, we should both have somewhere to go, something to do every day. So when we come home for dinner, we'll have plenty to talk about."

"We're moving in together?" Lilly was stunned. No one had ever asked her to move in with them. She was always the one suggesting, begging, sweet talking.

"I hate commuting between Santa Monica and Silver Lake. Besides . . ." Juliet took Lilly's hand. "I want to wake up with you every morning. I can't imagine you not being there in my bed."

"Really? Do you mean it?"

"Of course I mean it. I love you."

This is too much! Lilly thought. Between Juliet and Margaret and all this fantastic produce, I feel like I'm having a heart attack. Clutching her chest, she forced herself to breathe. I can't die now just when everything is getting really good.

On the way back to the car, they passed by the garish balloon man twisting up pink crowns for several dazed children.

"Isn't it amazing what he can do with those balloons?" said Juliet.

"Amazing," said Lilly. "You know, I just love that guy."

Chapter Twenty-Three

*R*ipping open the ivory linen envelope, Lauren
pulled out a sage-green invitation.

Please come for tea, it said in elegant black
script. *On Saturday, June 20th, at three o'clock.*

Down at the bottom was a spidery, handwritten note:
"Lauren, I apologize for my unprofessional behavior. Please
let me make it up to you. Margaret Moore."

"Fuck," she said.

"What?" said Dakota, not looking up from the television
screen.

"Margaret's having a 'Sorry I fired you' thing."

"It's all good."

"I guess." Kicking off her snakeskin sandals, Lauren
parked herself next to Dakota on the couch.

"I totally don't want to go. Hanging around, drinking tea with Clarissa? God."

Dakota didn't respond. He was tracking a sniper in *Jack This City*.

The party was a week from Saturday.

Yawning, she decided to wait and see if anything better came along.

Kate swapped out four tables and re-covered three chairs in bright raspberry cotton. She painted the tearoom walls a creamy lemon, replaced the landscapes with a collection of antique mirrors, and stripped the sagging chintz from the windows. It wasn't a severe make-over, but now Magpie's felt less like a cluttered attic and more like a favorite sitting room.

On Saturday afternoon, Margaret bought chocolate hazelnut truffles and ridiculously expensive artisan bread. She was in the kitchen, primping sandwiches, when Lilly turned up looking unusually gaudy in an embroidered tangerine silk tunic.

"Don't say anything! Juliet dressed me."

"You look lovely," said Margaret, stifling her laughter. "Go look at the room!"

The new decor met with Lilly's approval. Then, tying an apron over her tunic, she joined Margaret at the counter. "It's great. Kate's a genius."

Margaret smiled proudly as she gently mixed the egg salad.

Lilly stuck her finger in the bowl for a taste. "Needs more mayo," she said. "Did you add paprika?"

"There's a new jar in the pantry," said Margaret.

Lilly seized control of the egg salad, leaving Margaret to finish the scones and spoon out the Devon cream and jam. Preparing the meal together felt easy, like the roll of a favorite lipstick or driving down an empty boulevard at five o'clock.

Margaret stacked a tiered silver caddy with scones and truffles. "I thought we'd eat outside," she said, "take the terrace for a test drive."

A tall picket fence enclosed four mint-green wicker tables with bright glass tops. Against the outside wall, pink jasmine and rose vines climbed up a lattice.

Margaret frowned at the traffic. "It's bloody loud out here."

"People love noise," said Lilly. "No one in today's world can stand a moment of silence. If it's quiet they reach for their cell phones."

"This is fabulous," said Clarissa, sailing through the new French doors.

"I'm so glad you could come, dear," Margaret said, clasping Clarissa's hands. "What do you think? Is it too noisy?"

"No. This is a very trendy street. You could raise your prices."

Margaret herded them towards a table. "Please sit down while I fetch the tea."

"Shouldn't we wait for Lauren?" Clarissa's concern fooled no one.

"Oh, she's not coming," said Margaret. "She called a little while ago and said she was stuck in Malibu. Traffic was backed up on PCH, something of the sort."

"Oh, Malibu," said Lilly, snorting. "It's such a convenient excuse when you don't want to be somewhere."

Clarissa's shoulders relaxed. "That's too bad," she said with obvious relief.

Margaret sighed. "I hope the sacking didn't upset her too much."

"Oh, please," said Lilly. "She was late every single day she worked here!"

"Don't forget the lying . . . there's no way she could have had that many auditions," said Clarissa.

"Oh, all right. Perhaps we weren't terribly fond of her but . . . it is essential to be courteous and respectful, is it not?"

Lilly and Clarissa shared an exasperated look. "Not!" they said in unison.

Margaret scuttled back to the kitchen. Stealing a sideways glance at Clarissa, Lilly suddenly felt shy. They weren't, technically, friends, yet they knew so much of each other's intimate lives. She had witnessed Clarissa's nonstop tragedies and she supposed that Clarissa was dimly aware of her own pitiful love affairs.

"You look great," Lilly said.

"You, too," said Clarissa.

They wiggled awkwardly for a moment and then Lilly blurted out, "I'm in love! We're moving in together."

"Really? I'm seeing someone, too. My acting coach . . . well, my former coach—Vince—he's directing me in *Streetcar*. Getting fired was a positive experience for me. Really a gift . . ."

No conversational lulls with Clarissa, Lilly remembered wryly, as long as she's talking about herself.

". . . in life there are times when everything must burn to the ground before you can rise, like a Phoenix, from the flames."

"I pray we have all emerged triumphant from the ashes," said Margaret archly, setting down the pot. "I brewed the Cameroon. Clarissa, watch the tea while I retrieve the sandwiches."

"No, I'll get them," said Lilly, pulling Margaret down into a chair.

"Milk?" Margaret poised a small white pitcher over Clarissa's cup.

"Just a little."

Tipping the spout she said, "Tell me all about your class."

"You know how everyone always says teaching is rewarding?—well, it's really true! I feel so fulfilled as an acting coach. I didn't realize how much I had to give. And it is so important to pass the craft along to a new generation."

"Quite right! I hope they pay you well."

"Not yet. But, who knows? Maybe one day I'll have my own studio."

Lilly presented the silver caddy and a platter of dainty, crustless sandwiches to the table.

"I'm so glad you've found meaningful work." Margaret peeked into the pot, checking the color of the tea.

Clarissa helped herself to a small egg salad triangle, which she promptly cut in two. "And now that I'm so busy, I don't have time to worry about the business anymore."

There was the screech of brakes as out on 3rd, a Range Rover barely missed the rear end of a Jaguar.

"It's rather entertaining outside," Margaret said as they watched the blond in the Jaguar parallel park. "Oh, it's Carol Robman," she whispered. "Her mother-in-law's giving her a shower here next week."

Pitching her car two feet from the curb, Carol descended from the driver's seat and hefted her swollen belly over to their table. "Could you believe that Range Rover?" she said, looking extremely offended. "I nearly crashed the Jag."

We could believe it, they thought.

"Well, fuck her. I had to see the new tables." Carol lowered her sunglasses for the briefest of glances. "I love it! Thank god you're back. Where else could I go for little Preston's baby shower?"

"Lovely," said Margaret. "It will be the first party in our new room."

"Listen, about the sandwiches . . . I can't do salmon— you know, the whole toxic mercury thing. And I think there's a couple of vegans, so could you do an eggless egg salad?"

How perfectly ghastly! Margaret thought. What next?

Dairy-free Devon cream? She opened her mouth in dissent but Lilly sideswiped her.

"Faux-egg is no problem. Just call me—I'm Lilly the Chef—and we'll go over the menu."

Bracing her back with her hands, Carol pushed on. "Great. You know, I'm the last woman on the Westside to conceive. I've spent a fortune on gifts for everyone else's baby and now it's payback time."

Suddenly, Carol noticed Clarissa.

"Oh, my god. I've found Kit McCracken!"

"What?" Clarissa flinched.

"Didn't you used to be an actress?"

"Well, I'm still . . ."

"You were on *Russian Hill*, right?"

"*Detective Buck Love*."

Margaret and Lilly exchanged despairing glances.

"I remember you could really act. Not like these director's girlfriends that call themselves actors. I used to be in casting. Yes, you'd be the perfect Kit McCracken."

"Really?" said Clarissa, breathlessly. Then, "Who is . . ."

"One of the leads in my husband's pilot. Mid-season replacement."

Whipping out her cell phone, Carol speed-dialed. "Honey, I'm sitting right here with . . . what was your name again?"

"Clarissa Richardson."

"Melissa Richardson. Remember her from *Russian Hill*?"

"*Detective Buck Love*."

"She's your Kit. I'm never wrong—trust my instincts. Okay. I'll give her Bonnie's number. Don't forget Prenatal Therapy. Seven-thirty." She pushed end call and shrugged dramatically. "I should have been a producer. Then I'd see him more often."

Scrolling through contacts, she highlighted a number and stuck the screen in Clarissa's face. "Here's Bonnie, she's casting. Tell her Carol Robman said you're Kit."

Scooping a pen from her purse, Clarissa carefully wrote the number on a crumpled dry cleaning bill. "Thank you so much. I'm really grateful that you'd do this for me."

"No problem. I look at you and I see the world I left behind," said Carol, hugging her tummy. "And thank god! Preston is my ticket out of there. See you guys on the twenty-eighth. The Saturday before my Cesarean!"

Once properly stowed in the driver's seat, Carol swerved out in front of a hulking black pickup, whose driver leaned on the horn and flipped her off.

The tea party was momentarily speechless.

Oh, dear, thought Margaret gloomily. I expect the remainder of our afternoon will be spent soothing Clarissa's nerves while she frets about this audition. And why did I think outdoor tables were a good idea? These frightful drivers, the noise! The pollution!

Fuck me, thought Lilly.

"Wow," said Clarissa, helping herself to a warm currant scone. "I have been having the most amazing luck lately."

Like hawks, Margaret and Lilly watched for signs of anxiety.

Dotting the tiniest bit of clotted cream onto her plate, Clarissa smiled. "I can't wait to tell Vince. He'll help me with that audition. And he said I can use his agent if I book something."

Margaret and Lilly exhaled cautiously.

"My dear," said Margaret, patting Clarissa on the arm, "he sounds absolutely brilliant."

"Clarissa, you seem so strong," Lilly purred. "You know, I love that in a woman."

"Ladies," said Margaret crisply. "The leaves are perfectly steeped. Shall I pour the tea?"

The New Magpie's Tearoom

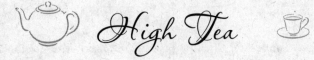

High Tea

— Choice of Tea —

English Breakfast: The classic blend of Assam, Ceylon, and Chinese leaves. Perfect with milk.

Earl Grey: Smoky and distinctive. Flavored with oil of Bergamot.

Cameroon: An African specialty, malty and aromatic. Served in the Court of England.

Jasmine: Silvery and elegant, with fragrant floral notes.

Chamomile: Calming and soothing. Best with lemon and honey.

Chai: Black tea and milk spiced with cardamom, coriander, and cloves.

Sandwiches

Cucumber and Sweet Butter, Watercress Dill, Egg Salad,
Prosciutto and Asparagus, Chicken Curry, Burrata and
Heirloom Tomato, Tofu Avocado*

Scones

Your choice of Traditional or Cranberry-Nut Scones
served with Devon Cream and Strawberry Jam

Sweets

Dulce de Leche Cake, Lemon Tart, Buttery Shortbread,
Chocolate Cupcakes with White Chocolate Frosting,
Panna Cotta with Caramelized Rose Petals*, locally
grown seasonal berries

*Non-Dairy

Featured Recipes
from the Tearoom . . .
and Elsewhere

The Perfect Cup of Tea

Sitting down with a cup of tea is truly one of life's pleasures.

YOUR CHOICE OF BLACK OR HERBAL TEA LEAVES
FRESHLY BOILED WATER
2-CUP TEAPOT

First, warm the teapot by filling it with hot water, then emptying this out.

Spoon 2 teaspoons of tea into a tea ball or tea sock, and place in pot.

Add 2 cups freshly boiled water. Allow to steep for 3 to 5 minutes for black tea; 7 minutes for herbal. No longer, otherwise the brew turns bitter. Remove ball or sock and pour tea into cup.

Sip and savor.

Can be used to relax, re-energize, reflect, or restore. It's just that good.

Egg Salad

Eggs go in and out of fashion, but they'll always be on the menu at Magpie's.

A DOZEN HARD-BOILED EGGS
A TON OF MAYO
PAPRIKA
SALT AND PEPPER
FRESH WHITE BREAD, THINLY SLICED

Mash up eggs with a ton of mayo. (Make sure it's Best Foods or Hellman's, not the fat-free stuff.)

Add paprika and salt and pepper and taste continually till right.

Slather over fresh bread and top with more bread. Cut into triangles.

Don't serve to egg-eschewers.

Cucumber Sandwiches

―――――――――

Cucumber sandwiches are elegant as well as comforting. As an added benefit, you may use any remaining slices for an impromptu spa treatment (see below).

UNSALTED BUTTER, SOFTENED
4 SLICES SOFT WHITE BREAD
1 ENGLISH CUCUMBER, THINLY SLICED
SALT AND PEPPER

Spread softened butter over the bread. Arrange cucumber over 2 slices and sprinkle with salt and pepper. Top with the remaining bread and cut corner to corner like an X. This will yield 8 small triangles, each with a handy crust on one side with which to hold the sandwich.

This will serve two for tea. If you're planning on lunch, you'd better add egg salad and cake or scones.

Place any remaining cucumber slices over tired or puffy eyes and lie down for a catnap.

Magpie's Scones

As with many treasured recipes, Margaret has changed this so many times it bears no resemblance to the original. No matter. She still thinks of it as her family heirloom.

2 CUPS UNBLEACHED FLOUR

1/4 CUP SUGAR PLUS MORE FOR SPRINKLING

1 TEASPOON BAKING POWDER

1/4 TEASPOON BAKING SODA

1/4 TEASPOON SALT

1 STICK COLD, UNSALTED BUTTER, CUT INTO SMALL
    PIECES

1/2 CUP BUTTERMILK (SLIGHTLY LESS ON RAINY
    DAYS, MORE ON DRY ONES)

1 EGG BEATEN WITH A LITTLE MILK TO THIN

Preheat the oven to 400°F.

Combine the dry ingredients in a food processor and whirl. Add butter and pulse until mixture resembles cornmeal.

Dump mixture into a large bowl and add buttermilk. Mix with your hands and form a lovely ball of dough.

Pat the dough into a circle. Cut the circle in half. Cut each half into 3 wedges.

Brush scones with egg wash and sprinkle liberally with sugar.

Bake on parchment-lined baking sheet for 17 minutes or until golden brown.

Serve warm with good cheer, Devon cream, and strawberry jam.

Lauren's Favorite Coffee Drink

Drive to current hippest coffee bar.

Order complex espresso drink (nonfat, caramel, sugar free, extra shot with whipped cream).

Strike up conversation with barista. (Who are you studying with now? Vince DeFaria? I think I've heard of him.)

Mention you're on Facebook.

Cap and sleeve drink.

Check out hot clientele on terrace.

Enjoy coffee with cigarette to complete meal.

Lilly's Breakfast Meeting Coffee Cake

Lilly says the key to a successful breakfast meeting is glaze.

1 STICK UNSALTED BUTTER, SOFTENED, PLUS SOME
    FOR COATING PAN

1 CUP GRANULATED SUGAR

2 EGGS

1 CUP SOUR CREAM

1 TEASPOON VANILLA EXTRACT

2 CUPS UNBLEACHED FLOUR

1 1/2 TEASPOONS BAKING POWDER

1/2 TEASPOON SALT

1 TEASPOON BAKING SODA

Streusel

1/3 CUP GOLDEN BROWN SUGAR

1 TEASPOON CINNAMON

1 TEASPOON FLOUR

1 CUP CHOPPED NUTS

Glaze

1 CUP CONFECTIONERS' SUGAR

1/4 CUP MAPLE SYRUP

Preheat the oven to 350°F. Grease and flour a Bundt pan.
With mixer, cream together the butter and sugar until light

and fluffy. Beat in the eggs, one at a time until combined. Mix in the sour cream and vanilla. In a separate bowl, sift together the flour, baking powder, salt, and baking soda. Add the flour mixture to the batter and stir until just combined.

To make the streusel, combine the brown sugar, cinnamon, 1 teaspoon flour, and nuts in a bowl.

Scoop half the batter into the prepared pan and spread it out with back of spoon or spatula. Sprinkle half the streusel mixture over. Spoon remaining batter into pan, and scatter rest of streusel over, patting it down.

Bake for 40 to 45 minutes until a cake tester comes out clean. Cool on rack. Unmold cake onto platter.

For the glaze, whisk the confectioners' sugar and maple syrup together, adding teaspoons of water to make it silky.

Lovingly drizzle glaze over cake, stand back, and let the forks fly.

Deborah's No-Eat Waffles

The ones that Deborah won't touch ... but Juliet will.

1 CUP FLOUR

1 TABLESPOON BROWN SUGAR

1 TEASPOON BAKING POWDER

1/2 TEASPOON BAKING SODA

1/4 TEASPOON SALT

1 EGG

1 CUP BUTTERMILK

A LITTLE MILK

2 TABLESPOONS MELTED BUTTER, PLUS MORE FOR
    COATING PAN

In a large bowl, combine all the dry ingredients. In a separate bowl, whisk the egg, buttermilk, a little milk, and butter. Add the liquid ingredients to the dry, stirring just until blended.

The batter should be the consistency of heavy cream; if it's not, thin with more milk.

Heat a waffle iron. Coat with more melted butter and ladle batter onto hot surface. Cook until golden brown and fragrant.

Lilly likes to serve these on Sunday mornings with fresh-squeezed orange juice, warm maple syrup, and the radio tuned to *This American Life*.

Lilly's Lobster, Avocado, and Corn Salad

Rich. Creamy. Sensuous. This is how Lilly spoils her lovers.

BEAUTIFUL MIXED GREENS SUCH AS MÂCHE, BABY
SPRING, OR ARUGULA
COOKED LOBSTER MEAT
1 AVOCADO, SLICED
KERNELS SLICED FROM 1 EAR WHITE CORN
2 TABLESPOONS OLIVE OIL
1 SHALLOT, MINCED
1 TABLESPOON CHAMPAGNE VINEGAR
SALT AND PEPPER

Place washed greens on two plates. Arrange lobster, sliced avocado, and corn over lettuce. Whisk together olive oil, shallot, vinegar, and salt and pepper to taste. Drizzle over salad.

Because of the seductive nature of this dish, it's best not to serve it to anyone you don't really, really like.

A lot.

Juliet's Spinach Frittata

Juliet says that if you can't master spinach frittata, you simply cannot run a bed and breakfast inn.

3 TABLESPOONS OLIVE OIL

2 GARLIC CLOVES, MINCED

1 BUNCH SPINACH, WASHED, BLANCHED, SQUEEZED
DRY, AND CHOPPED

8 EGGS

2 CUPS GRATED CHEESE (SHARP CHEDDAR, PARME-
SAN, GRUYÈRE, OR MIXTURE OF ALL THREE)

SALT AND PEPPER

Preheat the broiler.

Heat the olive oil in a medium, ovenproof skillet over low heat. Add the garlic and sauté until fragrant, about 1 minute. Mix in the spinach.

Whisk the eggs in a bowl with salt and pepper to taste. Pour over the spinach mixture in pan, stirring gently to blend. Cover the pan and cook until eggs are almost set, about 8 minutes.

Uncover the pan and sprinkle cheese over eggs. Slide under the broiler until cheese melts and bubbles. Watch so it doesn't burn.

Unmold the frittata onto a platter, or serve hot from the pan.

May be eaten before or *après* lovemaking, as it will stay perfectly delicious at room temperature for hours.

Pamela's Coconut Mojito

Most effective if knocked back in boisterous bar with dearest old friend.

COCONUT FLAKES

LEAVES FROM 4 OR 5 MINT SPRIGS

JUICE OF HALF A LIME

1 TEASPOON SUGAR

AS-MUCH-AS-IS-PRUDENT COCONUT RUM

Swirl the rim of a frosty, festive glass in coconut flakes, then fill with crushed ice. In a cocktail shaker, muddle mint, lime juice, and sugar, add as-much-as-is-prudent rum, and shake vigorously. Pour into prepared glass and serve with a saucy wink.

Repeat 2x while spilling guts, embellishing stories, and laughing uncontrollably.

Caution: Do not drive home. Do not make plans for the next day.

Margaret's Ex-Husband Roast Chicken

A roast chicken is simple, comforting, and devoid of conflict . . . the perfect dish for an ex-husband.

ONE 4-POUND CHICKEN

OLIVE OIL

1 TABLESPOON CHOPPED FRESH THYME, PLUS
    ADDITIONAL SPRIGS

SALT AND PEPPER

4 WHOLE GARLIC CLOVES

1 LEMON, SLICED

Preheat the oven to 400°F.

Place the chicken in a shallow roasting pan. Rub olive oil over skin, and sprinkle with chopped thyme, salt, and pepper. Scatter 2 garlic cloves and a few lemon slices in pan, drizzling them with oil. Place thyme sprigs and remaining lemon and remaining garlic cloves inside cavity.

Roast until golden brown and juices run clear, about 1 hour.

Serve with buried hatchet to ex-husband and his new partner.

Clarissa's No-Fail Soup

Open kitchen cupboard.

Remove can of soup (low-fat, 90 calories per serving).

Dump into small saucepan.

Heat on stove.

Pour into bowl.

Carry to living room.

Sip slowly while watching reruns of *Law & Order.*

Tony's Pork Medallions

This is Tony's signature dish . . . and Margaret taught him how to make it.

4 BONELESS, WAFER-THIN PORK MEDALLIONS
SALT AND PEPPER
2 TABLESPOONS UNSALTED BUTTER
2 TABLESPOONS OLIVE OIL
1 TABLESPOON CHOPPED FRESH THYME
2 GARLIC CLOVES, MINCED
3 TABLESPOONS RED WINE VINEGAR
1/2 CUP CHICKEN STOCK
SPLASH OF WHATEVER YOU'RE DRINKING
MORE BUTTER
FRESH THYME SPRIGS

Season the pork with salt and pepper. Melt 2 tablespoons butter and olive oil in a large skillet. Add the medallions and sauté briefly, until just cooked through, about 2 minutes per side. Remove to large platter and cover with foil to keep warm.

Add the chopped thyme and garlic to pan. Cook for 1 minute. Add the vinegar, scraping up all of those lovely charred meat bits. Mix in broth and a splash of whatever you're drinking. Simmer until the sauce is reduced, 2 to 3 minutes, then stir in more butter.

Return the pork to skillet and heat through.

Arrange. the medallions on a platter with the sauce. Garnish with thyme sprigs and serve to guests with dramatic flair.

Margaret's Fine Beef Stew

This is something to consider when you have hours of time stretching before you, it's raining, and there's nowhere to go.

3 POUNDS BEEF STEW MEAT
FLOUR
SALT AND PEPPER TO TASTE
OLIVE OIL
1 LARGE ONION, CHOPPED
BEEF BROTH
RED WINE
POTATOES AND CARROTS, CUT INTO CHUNKS
CHOPPED HERBS SUCH AS THYME, TARRAGON,
    OREGANO (YOUR PREFERENCE)

Dust the meat with flour, and sprinkle with salt and pepper to taste. Heat olive oil in a heavy, ovenproof pot. Sauté the beef in batches (don't crowd) till browned. Remove to platter. Heat more oil and sauté the onion till soft. Return the beef to pot; pour in broth and wine to cover and place the pot in the oven on a low temperature, say, 325°F. The lower you go, the longer it will take to cook, so you can stretch this part out for the entire afternoon if it's a particularly gloomy day.

About two hours in, add potatoes, carrots, and herbs of choice. Stir it all and return pot to oven till vegetables and meat are tender, another hour or so.

Serve with pride . . . a fine beef stew is utterly delicious and quite an accomplishment in a world of fifteen-minute meals.

Evelyn's Toast

Served every morning in Shropshire.

1 SLICE WHOLE WHEAT BREAD
ICE COLD BUTTER
MARMALADE

Toast your whole wheat bread until dark brown.

Cut in half.

Place triangles in silver toast rack and carry to breakfast table.

Allow toast to grow stone cold.

Spread icy butter across brittle surface.

Top with marmalade.

Alternate crunches of toast with sips of tea.

Kevin the Handyman's
Breakfast, Lunch, and Dinner

———

He's a regular at the seedy, lime-green stand on Fairfax.

CHILI CHEESE DOG WITH ONIONS
LARGE FRIES WITH MAYO AND KETCHUP
EXTRA-LARGE MOUNTAIN DEW

Order to go.
Scarf dog in van en route to job.
Toss greasy bag and leftover fries into back seat.
Marinate garbage for months to infuse vehicle with rank, noxious odor.